tin grin

REASONS FOR KILLING RUPERT:

1) *He is completely insensitive*
2) *He enjoys showing people up in public*
3) *He is a total embarrassment*
4) *He can't dance to save his life*
5) *He has no dress sense whatsoever (unless helped by an adult)*
6) *He has a superiority complex*
7) *He has an irritating voice*
8) *He's getting zits (HA HA HA)*
9) *He's a specky four-eyed metal-mouthed dwarf…*
10) *…and a smug little git to boot*
11) *He's a psychotic axe-murderer*
12) *He farts in public*
13) *and picks his nose ditto*
14) *and wets his bed*
15) *He smells*

I was well aware that items 7) to 15) were either not his fault, not true, or simply me being immature, but I did-

Scholastic Children's Books,
Commonwealth House, 1-19 New Oxford Street
London WC1A 1NU, UK

A division of Scholastic Ltd
London ~ New York ~ Toronto ~ Sydney ~ Auckland
Mexico City ~ New Delhi ~ Hong Kong

First published in the UK by Scholastic Ltd, 2001

ISBN 0 439 99615 5

Typeset by TW Typesetting, Midsomer Norton, Somerset
Printed by Cox & Wyman Ltd, Reading, Berks.

1 2 3 4 5 6 7 8 9 10

chapter one

According to official sources, whatever they might be, you're more likely to fail at school, not get a job, do drugs and drop out – in other words, be what they call dysfunctional – if you come from a single-parent family.

Yeah, I thought that would make you stop and think. It made me stop and think, too. It made me stop and think what a load of crap these so-called official sources spout. I mean to say, who is it they use as case studies? Is it their idea of the typical one-parent family – mum of about sixteen, with three kids under three, living on a drug-ridden, rat-infested council estate, with no men and unemployment levels of about eighty per cent? Or is it real people, from real families?

We all know them. They're in all our streets, all our classes, all our families. My mate Jaz did a survey once, for Social Studies. She found out that, in our class of twenty-nine, only twelve kids lived with both their natural parents, who were married to each other. Twelve out of twenty-nine, living in the Official Sources' idea of the proper family set-up. If you ask me, there's only one kid in our year going down the road to dysfunction, and that's Bradley Smythe. Brad Smythe, trainee junkie and Prat of the Year: and he's one of the twelve. So there you go, Official Sources – take that bit of research, and do what you like with it.

Of course, I'm not exactly what you might call unbiased. Up until recently, I was one of the other seventeen, from the Lone Parent Brigade. Me and Molly and Mum, all as happy as can be. The move from Manchester down to Devon was a bit of a wrench at the time, for me. At ten, your friends are beginning to be really important. But I soon made new ones, as Mum said I would. Molly didn't care – she was only seven, and at that age everything is a Huge Adventure. And unhappy though I was at leaving all my mates behind, I was old enough to realize that anything was better than staying where we were. With Dad. Even Molly was old enough to realize that.

Dad used to beat Mum up. He was away a lot, working. I'm not sure what he did – didn't care, still don't – but when he came back the pattern was the same. Dump suitcase, big kiss for Mum – down the pub, big smack around the face for Mum. It never varied. Oh, except the once. That was when I, all ten years and

2

four feet nine of me, decided I was going to do the super-hero bit, and started laying into him. I say laying into – I must have come up to about his kneecaps. Dumb, or what? Anyway, the upshot was that I got a big smack around the face as well, and *that* was when Mum decided enough was enough, and we up-sticked (or whatever the expression is) to North Devon.

Or so she says. To tell the truth, I don't really remember much of that time. Don't want to, either. All I know is, it felt great when we moved down here. Mum found this damp little cottage in the middle of nowhere, on a steep private lane to a small stony cove, and Molly and I thought we were in heaven, not Devon (ha ha). Bit of a change from the middle of Manchester; our surroundings couldn't have been more different if we'd moved to Outer Mongolia, or the moon. Mum said she'd always hated city life, and the solitude and peace of the cottage and the countryside was good for her chi (actually, she said it was good for all our chis, but I'm not sure I've got one).

Anyway. Down here we came, and down here we remain, five years on. Gradually we settled in: Mum got the damp in the cottage fixed, and had a bit built on to the back so Moll and I had a room each. There were new schools for us, and new friends. Mum got a job – something to do with Art and Design at the University. And for the first time since I could remember, she looked happy. Not hunted, or haunted, or constantly checking the calendar to see when Dad was due home next. We were all happy. I didn't miss Dad at all – well, perhaps just a tiny bit, but then you do miss a headache once it's gone, don't you? You notice the absence of pain, and the resulting lightness of spirits, and you wonder how you managed to put up with it for so long.

In short, life was pretty damn fine. Until last year. Last year, everything changed for good. The cosy, private little world that we had painstakingly built together, Mum and Molly and me, out of the grotesque caricature of family life we'd had before with Dad – all that was over. Gone, finished, kaput. Because last year, Geoffrey came into our lives, and what was worse – a hundred times worse – he brought Rupert with him.

To begin with, I didn't really take much notice when Mum started going out more in the evenings. I knew there was a man involved, she'd never been at all devious or secretive about that, but she'd gone out with the occasional man before; it had never bothered me in the past and it didn't bother me then. I'm not one of those precious, clingy daughters who resent their mothers having a social life and going out with — shock, horror — *men*. Truth to tell, I quite liked it. I thought Mum was pretty cool, and I liked the fact that men seemed to think so too. I thought she deserved to have fun, after the rubbish life she'd had with Dad, and I suppose I was glad to see her having some at last. Not that a couple of drinks of an evening with some of the drongos she trips over at work was *my* idea of fun, mind, but there you go. I'm not thirty-nine.

Put like that, I sound really condescending, don't I? I don't mean to be. I genuinely didn't have a problem with Mum going out with men, not even when she brought one or two of them home for supper (or, as I later recognized, to sound me and Moll out about them). The Stevens and the Rogers came and went, and Molly and I smiled sweetly at them and passed the bread, and answered their polite, well-intentioned questions about school and hobbies and what we wanted to be when we grew up, and all I felt was a faint sense of pride that Mum — *my mum* — was, I don't know, joining the human race again. Worthy of being something to a man other than a human punch-bag. I loved her, you see. Still do, of course, but things are different now. She doesn't need me to look out for her any more.

What Molly made of all this, heaven only knows. We never discussed it: well, you don't discuss your mother's sex life with your kid sister, do you? But she seemed happy enough with her life and all it encompassed, including Mum's gentleman callers, to use an old-fashioned phrase.

I don't remember when the penny began to drop that Mum was getting serious about one of them. Perhaps I noticed that one man's name was being mentioned rather more often and for rather longer than any of the others. Or maybe I twigged that, despite weeks and weeks of Geoffrey this and Geoffrey that, we never seemed to get to meet him.

Whatever. What I do remember, and so vividly it raises the hair on the nape of my neck, even now, is the sensation I had when she did finally invite him over for the inspection supper.

At the time, there was no reason to suppose the evening was going to be any different from the handful of other occasions when the Gentleman Caller of the moment had been invited over. There was no big build-up. Mum hadn't cooked anything special: it was lasagne and salad, as I recall, with garlic bread out of a

6

packet, and fruit for pudding. I also remember that Mum hadn't had time to wash her hair beforehand, even though she'd come home intending to. She'd got engrossed in something, helping Molly or me with homework probably, and the time had slipped by, so she just swept her hair up and stuck a comb through it.

She hadn't had time to change, either. So when the doorbell rang (at exactly seven thirty, I remember that as well) I thought her uncharacteristic fluster was due to being unprepared for her guest.

She came back from answering the door followed by a shadowy figure, hovering in the sitting-room doorway.

"This is Geoffrey Horton," she said, and stood to one side so we could have a better look.

He was immensely tall and thin, with greying dark hair and thick, horn-rimmed specs. He was dressed in shabby dark-brown cord trousers and a baggy cardigan the colour of dust, and as he stuck out his right hand I could see a fraying shirt cuff above his bony wrist.

"Hello," he said, taking a step forward.

He was everyone's idea of the archetypal university professor. Unkempt, untrendy and utterly, utterly unprepossessing. *Boy oh boy*, I thought. *What on earth has Mum found now?*

7

No I didn't. I'm lying. At that stage, when we first met, I had completely different views about him. The bad stuff came later; I shouldn't pretend otherwise. That first evening, I liked him. I thought he looked nice. Scruffy, but nice. His clothes might have looked as if they came from Oxfam (they probably did, come to that), but his eyes behind his specs were warm and brown and mild. He had that slight stoop very tall people often have, but on him it didn't look apologetic, but rather as if he was leaning towards you to catch your every fascinating word. And he had a friendly, lopsided smile, and a kindly air about him.

"Hello," I said back, and shook his hand. I shot a glance at Mum, and that's when it happened.

Two things.

1) Mum had this odd look on her face — proud, proprietorial. And it wasn't pride in introducing us, her daughters, but in him: the new man in her life. She had a kind of glow around her. Ready Brek Woman. She'd say it was her aura, but it wasn't. She was glowing with happiness and pride and contentment and … oh, and all kinds of things I couldn't put a name to, and still can't. I'd never seen her look like that before.

2) A voice in my head said, "She's going to marry him." Yeah, yeah, I know. Voices in my

head: it sounds about as likely as auras and chi. But I know what I heard, and what I saw too, and how those things made me feel.

All the hairs on the back of my neck stood on end. I took a step back, it was quite involuntary, and I suppose I must have looked odd or made a strange noise, some little gasp or something, because Mum said, "Are you all right, darling?"

"Yes, I'm fine."

Well, what else could I say? Why are you all lit up like a Christmas tree, and when's the wedding?

I felt like a bit of a prat, to be honest. There was absolutely nothing out of the ordinary about that evening, no obvious signs like them holding hands under the table or snogging in the kitchen when our backs were turned. Nothing. And Molly didn't pick up on anything, that's for sure. Afterwards, when he'd gone, I asked her what she'd thought of him.

"Of who?" she said. She looked totally blank.

"Tinky Winky, of course, who else?" I tutted impatiently. "Come on, Moll. Who d'you think I mean? Geoffrey Horton. The man we've just eaten supper with. Mum's latest fanciable."

She frowned slightly. She's very fastidious, is Moll. "That's not very nice. He's not Mum's latest fanciable, he's just one of the Nigels."

That was our name for them, the men Mum

had met at work (usually) and brought home for our inspection. The Nigels. That had been the name of the first, Nigel Meredith, and there had been three or four since, all of whom we collectively called the Nigels. We hadn't meant anything by it, nothing insulting. I guess it felt more appropriate to us than calling them "Mum's boyfriends". It seemed ridiculous to call men in their forties "boyfriends", but quite apart from that, it had been obvious, even to us, that the relationship between Mum and each of the Nigels had simply been one of friendship.

But this time, things were different. Whatever else Geoffrey Horton might be to Mum — or was going to be — one of the Nigels he wasn't. I didn't say that to Molly, though. How could I? She'd have thought I'd cracked, or was imagining things. I even half-thought that myself, at the time. Which only goes to show that you should trust your instincts when it comes to first impressions.

Geoffrey was an archaeologist, a specialist in Iron Age Celtic burial sites or something equally riveting. He had taken up a professorship at the local university at the beginning of that academic year, a *chair* as they are rather bizarrely called. He had started there in late

September or early October, and I guess it must have been February or March by the time Molly and I finally got to meet him.

So although it seemed to us that their relationship moved on pretty rapidly after that supper (the one when I heard prophetic voices), in reality they'd already known each other for five or six months.

"It doesn't matter how long I've known him," Mum told us. "You know when you meet someone special. It's not a question of time."

Even with her admitting that Geoffrey was special, it didn't bother me that much. Oh sure, I'd have probably preferred her to be seeing someone a bit more presentable, given the choice. A bit more *mainstream*. Somebody who didn't have the sartorial sense of a scarecrow, and with a slightly less boffy job – like a film producer, say, or an A&R man for a top record label. That would have been cool. Unlikely, but cool. But Geoffrey was OK, in a deeply unhip, kindly-uncle-figure sort of way.

So anyway, there we were, in a routine with old Geoffrey coming round once or twice a week, and Mum going over there about the same amount, and drifting around in-between times with a dippy smile on her face. He never stayed over and I know for a fact Mum didn't stay the night there either, so they couldn't have had much of a physical side to their relationship if you know what I mean, and I'm sure you do. The most they seemed to get up to was a sneaky, teenagey holding-of-hands on the sofa, listening to one of Mum's weird Mood Music CDs.

The reason I'm telling you all this is to try and convey the sense of shock I had when Mum dropped her bombshell one evening about Geoffrey's son.

"Oh, by the way," she said, trying to be casual but failing miserably, "Geoffrey's bringing his son round when he comes on Sunday. We thought it was about time you kids met each other."

Loaded statement, or what? I was so astonished – so astounded, so *gobsmacked* – all I could do was stare at her. There was so much subtext in that seemingly innocent little remark: like, how come she'd been seeing Geoffrey for weeks and this was the first time a son had been mentioned? Like, why was it about time we met him? And what was with all this "oh, by the way" stuff, trying to be cool and laid-back and pretending it was no big deal?

I knew perfectly well it *was* a big deal. Geoffrey's son entering the picture could only mean one thing: that their relationship was shifting up a gear, from the casual supper-twice-a-week that I was comfortable with, to something much more official and long-term.

But even then — *even then* — I think I could have got used to the idea. Supported it, even. But that was before I met Rupert.

chapter two

Oh man. What can I say about Rupert? What can I tell you that isn't going to make you feel instantly, permanently sorry for him, the poor motherless little soul, and damn me to everlasting hell for being such an insensitive, bullying cow?

All I can say is, it wasn't like that at the time. Whatever happened later – and I put my hands up to that, I take my fair share of the blame, which is probably about ninety per cent, I admit it – whatever went on subsequently, our initial meeting wasn't exactly what you might call auspicious. It rather set the tone for the future. And *that*, as you will find out, was hardly my fault.

It wasn't that I deliberately set out to dislike him. *Au contraire*, as Jaz would say. Once I'd got over the shock of Geoffrey having a son and heir I hadn't known about, I felt quite sorry for him. Not for being Geoffrey's son, I don't mean that; but because I knew (Mum had told us) that Geoffrey's wife had died a year or so ago.

14

"Blimey, he hasn't wasted any time then, has he?" I couldn't help it: it just kind of slipped out.

Mum looked faintly pained. "Don't be unkind, Mattie. She'd been ill for ages. Geoffrey had been coping more or less on his own for almost three years before we met. He doesn't feel it's too soon for another woman's presence in his life, and I have to say neither do I. He's really not the sort of man who functions well by himself."

You're not kidding, I thought, remembering the frayed cuffs, but didn't say so.

"So how old is this kid, then?"

"Thirteen. He's between you and Molly in age, which is rather nice, we think."

Why was it nice? What possible connection could his age have with ours? And why didn't that little comment set the alarm bells ringing in my brain? Or maybe it did, subliminally. Maybe Mum's little throw-away remarks and my barely registered perceptions all added up in my mind. How am I supposed to know? I'm not a psychiatrist.

What I'm trying to say here is, I'm pretty sure I had no preconceptions or pre-formed judgements of what Rupert was going to be like before he turned up on the doorstep with his father, on that sunny Sunday afternoon at

15

the beginning of the May half-term holiday.

They came for tea, which in my opinion was a mistake in itself. Mum doesn't really do tea, not being much of a cake-baker. Much as I love her, I'm not convinced that carob-coated oat bars rate very high in the how-to-impress-the-new-man's-son stakes. Ten minutes before they were due to arrive, I came downstairs to find her in the kitchen, trying to melt carob bars on the unhelpful and sulky Aga.

"Are you sure about this?" I asked her.

"What do you mean?"

"Well, *carob*..." I trailed off. "Are there tofu sandwiches as well?"

Mum clapped a distracted hand to her head. "Sandwiches! I totally forgot about sandwiches. What on earth can I put in them?" She threw open one of the cupboards and began rifling around in it. "I think there's some tahini in here somewhere..."

Molly and I exchanged glances. "Mum," I began.

"Mmm?" She took out a sticky jar of Marmite with *Best before end April 1990* stamped on the lid. "Oh dear. I don't think this will do, do you?"

"No, I don't. I don't think your average thirteen-year-old is into tahini and prehistoric Marmite." I could feel myself going into taking-over mode – it's a failing of mine. "Why doesn't Molly boil some eggs for egg mayonnaise, and I'll go to the shop and see if they've got any peanut butter?"

"Would you, love? That would be helpful." She turned to find her purse. "Oh, and you'd better get some bread, too. There's only a couple of slices left."

It's a couple of kilometres to the shop, and most of that's uphill, but I don't mind – I'm used to it. I took Molly's bike, musing as I did so that only my mother could invite people for tea and then realize, five minutes beforehand, that there was nothing to feed them with.

The shop had run out of bread but they did have some packets of white rolls (a treat: shop-bought white bread is normally outlawed in our house) so I bought those instead. I also found the peanut butter, eight chocolate éclairs and two packets of chocolate biscuits. *Stuff carob*, I thought, freewheeling down the hill with my legs stuck straight out, *let's OD on the real thing for a change*.

As I turned the corner by the cottage I very nearly collided with a grey Volvo estate. Geoffrey – with offspring. I gave an airy wave and sprinted the last few metres, throwing the bicycle down in the drive and racing indoors with the food.

"They're here," I puffed. "Go and let them in!"

But before anyone could move there was a tap on the back door, and into the kitchen came Geoffrey with his son.

Clones. That was my first, immediate thought. The boy was a miniature version of his father. Pipe-cleaner skinny; bony wrists. Same dark hair, same brown eyes behind the same specs. Same pallid complexion – as if they had both spent their lives locked in a windowless room.

There were differences, of course. Father's hair was springy and flecked with grey, whereas son's was black as a raven's wing and combed savagely flat, with a precision-ruled centre parting. Geoffrey was tall, beanpole height, but his son was small for his age, shorter than Molly despite being a year older. And his face was solemn, deadpan, lacking his father's gentle smile and kindly expression.

"Hello," said Geoffrey, with said smile and ditto expression. "I'd like you all to meet Rupert."

He was dressed like a forty year old, in a blazer (a blazer!) and too-short grey trousers, a white shirt and a tie (a *tie!*) with some kind of emblem or crest.

"How do you do," he said politely, and shook our hands in turn. As he spoke I could see he

18

had braces, the full set across top and bottom teeth.

"This is Alice Fry," Geoffrey told him, as he shook Mum's hand.

"How do you do, Mrs Fry."

"And this is Molly."

"How do you do."

"And this is Matilda."

"Mattie," I corrected him. "Hello, Rupert."

There was no "How do you do" for me. Instead, he looked up at me. Our eyes met. His were expressionless.

"Matilda Fry," he said. He couldn't quite pronounce his Rs: they caught on his bottom lip, and my name came out as Matilda Fwy. "My mother was called Matilda."

Past tense. His *dead* mother. What an opening gambit. How could I answer that? How lovely? How dreadful? It was only later it occurred to me it was probably deliberate, designed to wrong-foot not just me, but everyone in the room.

Geoffrey gave a nervous little laugh. He was clearly embarrassed, although he hadn't gone red or anything. (That's my speciality.)

"That's right," he said, rather too loudly. "She was always known as Tilda, though," he said to the room, "which is quite different from Mattie, isn't it?"

My mother stood quite still. All the welcoming hustle and bustle had gone from her. She said, "You never told me that, Geoffrey. What an extraordinary coincidence."

"Yes." He rubbed his hands together in a not altogether successful attempt at heartiness. "My goodness me, look at all this wonderful food. You're spoiling us, Alice."

I followed Rupert's gaze down to the kitchen table, littered as it was with half-shelled hard-boiled eggs, extinct tubs of Marmite, lime pickle and tahini, and the ruins of the carob bars. Then he looked at Mum, appraising her. She was wearing the fringed purple skirt she'd bought at Glastonbury two years ago, with a hand-woven hemp shirt and her new patchwork waistcoat. Her Guatemalan silver earrings dangled practically to her shoulders; she had yin and yang pendants and crystals on leather thongs around her neck, and exotic mehndi patterns painted in henna on the backs of her hands and snaking up her arms. (I'd helped her apply them two nights before: they were connected with some project on Asian body art she was working on at the university.)

Rupert took it all in. Then his mouth stretched into a stiff social smile that didn't reach his eyes and was a curious mixture of disgust and smugness.

"Wonderful," he said.

Jaz wasn't much help, when I told her about it back at school.

"He looked at Mum as if she was an alien."

"Well, you can see his point," she said.

I stared at her. "Gee, thanks."

"C'mon, Mattie. You know what I mean. Your mum is a bit…"

"A bit what?" I was on the defensive immediately.

"Exotic. Takes your breath away the first time you meet her."

"She didn't take *your* breath away."

"She did. I was just too polite to say so."

This time I just raised one eyebrow.

"Oh, Mat, come *on*! I love your mum, she's well cool, but you have to look at it from whatsisname's point of view."

"Rupert," I said, scathingly.

"Yeah, Rupert. Jeez, is that really his name? Was he wearing yellow trousers with black squares on?" She giggled.

"No, a nerdy blazer and his school tie."

It was her turn to stare. "You're joking. His school tie?" She fell silent for a moment, no doubt contemplating the monstrousness of the vision. "What school?" she asked, eventually.

I tutted. "Does it matter?"

"No, but—" She lifted a shoulder. "I just wondered."

"I can't remember its name. It's in Surrey somewhere. Or Berkshire. Somewhere like that. Somewhere Home Counties and posh. It's a boarding school."

"Oh, right. That explains it. I was wondering why he hadn't met your mum before, when she's been seeing his dad for months."

"Well, now you know. He's been away at school, and he came home for half-term and was toted round to meet us."

"So why's he meeting you all now? How come he didn't meet you all in the other holidays? Like, say, at Easter?"

"How am I supposed to know? Maybe Geoffrey kept us all from him, like a guilty secret. Maybe he thought Rupert's stomach wasn't strong enough to meet my mother before now. Who cares?"

The bell went for first lesson. Jaz humped her sack of school books on to her shoulder. "You know my birthday?"

She does this sometimes: changes the subject with mind-boggling speed.

"What?"

"My birthday." She sighed, and clicked her fingers in front of my nose. "Hello. Earth to Matilda. You remember birthdays? Jelly and ice

22

cream, and cakes with candles? Another year older, another year closer to the pub?"

"Yeah, yeah. Don't be sarky. What about it?"

"Dad says I can have a party."

"Wow."

"No, I mean it. A proper party. Not jelly and ice cream and stuff. A rave."

"A *rave*?" I couldn't imagine it. Jaz's father is an eye surgeon at a big teaching hospital, and a very upright citizen. He and raves go together like the Lone Ranger and Toronto.

"Well, perhaps not a *rave* rave. But not a kiddies' do. I want dancing and lasers and stuff." A sneaky look passed across her face. "And I'm going to ask Sam."

Sam! Be still, my beating heart. Sam Barker is a mega-hunk, in the year above us: I've had a secret crush on him for about a century. Or perhaps not so secret.

I tried to look nonchalant. "I'd come to your party whether Sam was there or not, Jaz. When is it?"

"Not sure yet. Beginning of the summer holidays, probably." Jaz's birthday is at the end of July; sometimes in term time, sometimes not.

"Great." I looked at my watch. "We'd better get a move on – Simkins will go ballistic if we're late for Maths again."

Something Jaz had said troubled me. It was the timing of the whole thing – not her birthday, but the Rupert thing. Why *had* he suddenly been brought round to meet us all, when we hadn't even known he existed until a couple of days before? If I hadn't known Mum better, I'd have thought she was up to something. But it was impossible: she is so transparently honest, so incapable of hiding things, I'd have known instantly if there had been any ulterior motive. I dismissed it all as coincidence. Mum had asked Geoffrey for tea, his son was home for half-term, so he came too. What could be less sinister than that?

I should have known better, of course. I should have trusted my instincts, again. When Molly and I got home from school, that very afternoon, there was Mum waiting in the kitchen for us, with Geoffrey and a bottle of wine. All of those things were unusual, to say the least: Mum is very rarely home before us, and she never brings Geoffrey with her. As for the wine, she is a strictly Christmas-and-birthdays-only drinker. But there she was, glugging Cava (sparkling wine, too; uh-oh) like she always hits the booze at half past four of an afternoon. My instincts went on red alert.

"What's going on?" I asked suspiciously.

Mum just smiled. I think she was trying to

look mysterious, but thanks to the wine she just looked faintly cross-eyed. She handed Molly and me a glass each, and Geoffrey poured in some of the fizz.

"We're celebrating," she said, smiling at him.

Molly glared at her. "Are you drunk?" she demanded.

"Of course I'm not drunk."

"Then what's all this about?" I waved my glass around, and a small tidal wave of wine swooshed over the edge.

"Oops," said Mum, and giggled.

"You *are* drunk," Molly declared.

"No I'm not. I'm just happy."

And then she told us that Geoffrey had asked her to marry him, and that she had said yes.

chapter three

Strangely enough, the real implications didn't actually hit me until Molly pointed them out later that evening, when Geoffrey had left and Mum was swanning round downstairs clutching the empty Cava bottle and humming "All You Need is Love". My mind was full of the wedding: would it be church (romantic, but a bit OTT at their age) or registry office (soulless but more appropriate)? Would Molly and I be expected to be bridesmaids? Would there be an evening do? And, if so, could I possibly find a way of inviting Sam that wouldn't end up with me being horribly embarrassed by a) my family and possibly, b) my bridesmaid's dress?

Then, "He'll be our stepfather," Molly announced, bursting into my room and flumping herself down on the bed. I was sitting at my desk, writing in my diary – which isn't really a diary at all but more of a kind of journal: I don't write in it every day, only when I feel like it. It doesn't contain the sort of earth-shatteringly exciting things Jaz writes in *her* diary, like *"cheese roll for lunch (340 cals), Eng.*

26

Lit. + Hist. homework (in by Tuesday), chicken jalfrezi + rice + chips, plum pie + ice cream for supper (1200 cals, must eat more fresh veg.)" I kid you not. She actually wrote that last week.

"Did you hear?" Molly asked. "He'll be our stepfather. Geoffrey."

I put my finger in the spine of the diary to stop it closing, and looked up.

"Oh, *duh*," I said. "Nothing much gets past you, does it?" And I went back to comparing the grossness of sprigged chintz versus slippery satin bridesmaid dresses.

"So we'll be called Horton," Molly went on, idly pleating the duvet cover between her fingers.

This time I didn't bother looking up. "No, we won't, drongo. Not unless he adopts us, which doesn't seem likely. Why would he want to adopt two daughters?"

"Yeah," said Molly, gloomily, "when he's already got a son. Course, *he'll* be our step-brother."

I dropped the pen on the floor and spun round on the swivel chair. "Christ!"

Molly looked startled. "What? What is it?"

"Wupert. I'd forgotten all about him."

Sniggering, Molly sat up and hugged her knees. "Wupert. I like it. Wupert!"

"No, but Moll…" I propelled the chair

27

urgently towards her across the carpet. "He's going to be our *stepbrother*. He's going to live here. With *us*!"

She stopped sniggering and nodded solemnly instead. "I know. Pants, isn't it?"

"Yes, but…" She didn't seem to have grasped the full horror of the situation. I gesticulated wildly under her nose. "There's only three bedrooms. One for them, one for us, one for him. We're going to have to share. One of us will have to give up our room for him."

Her whole body slumped. "Oh hell. I hadn't thought of that. But how d'you know they'll be living here? Maybe we'll go and live with them. I mean, they don't *have* to come here, do they?"

But I knew otherwise. "Yes they do. Geoffrey's got that rented flat near the university, remember? He told Mum what a squash it is when Rupert's home in the holidays. There's no way there'd be room there for all of us."

"Well, maybe they're going to buy somewhere bigger," she suggested, brightening. "And anyway, Rupert's away at school most of the time, isn't he? He won't be here much." She has this irritating tendency to look on the bright side, my sister. I could slap her sometimes.

"He'll be here enough. And I don't want them to get somewhere bigger. Do you? This is our home, here. *Our* home."

28

I was aware of speaking fiercely; possessively, proprietorially. It was weird — one moment I was calmly cataloguing the entire Laura Ashley bridal collection, the next I was seized with a passionate fury that I'd never felt before. Not even during those far-off days in Manchester. It didn't have much effect on Molly, though. Casting her eyes heavenwards in a long-suffering look, she just sighed, and slid off the bed.

"We'll just have to put up with it, won't we? Far as I can see, there's no choice. I'm going downstairs to watch *EastEnders*. See ya."

It got worse. It appeared that we were expected to share not only our home, but our school too. Following the wedding (August: school holidays), Rupert was to start at St Mark's with us in September.

"But why?" I wailed, when Mum told me. "What's wrong with his own school?"

"Nothing," she said. "But boarding school's not ideal, is it? Not when he doesn't have to board."

"Why doesn't he have to? I mean, why did he have to before, but not now?"

"Because things have changed now — or they will, after the wedding."

I pulled a face. "I still don't see why he has to

29

come to our school." I could just imagine my friends' faces when he came trotting along with Molly and me at the beginning of next term: meet my new stepbrother, the dweeb.

"It's not that he has to, exactly," said Mum, patiently. "He only started boarding at his school in January, when Geoffrey got the post here at Exeter. He's in his final year there, so starting at a new school then would have been pretty pointless; and Geoffrey thought it best for Rupert to stay in a familiar environment, especially with all the upheaval there'd been after his mother died. But he'd have been starting somewhere new round here in September anyway – Geoffrey only ever intended the boarding to be a temporary arrangement – and under the circumstances it makes sense for the three of you to go to school together."

"Won't manky old St Mark's be a bit of a come-down?" I said, moodily. "After a fancy prep school?"

Mum gave me a strange sideways glance. "It's not manky. And Rupert's school isn't fancy; at least, not from what I've heard of it. Don't be snobby, darling – it's not like you."

"Snobby?" I burst out. "I'm not snobby! Snobs don't go to common comprehensives like St Mark's – they go to *boarding school*!" I said the words in a fake posh accent, wondering as I did so why I was doing it. I had nothing against boarding schools – I'd barely even given them a thought before now. School was school, a necessary evil.

But Mum looked pained. "It's inverted snobbery, Mattie. It's just as bad as the other kind. Worse, maybe. Rupert went to that school because he's clever and got a scholarship, and he boarded for very good reasons."

Clever. Wouldn't you just know it. Not only was he going to show me up with his nerdy appearance, but he'd probably outshine me academically, too. Great. And now here was Mum, lecturing me on being a snob like I was ten years old.

"And there's another thing," I said, the bit well and truly between my teeth. "Just where's he going to sleep?"

Mum blinked. "Sorry?"

"Sleep; you know, what you do in a bedroom?"

Mum chewed on her bottom lip in a faintly discomfited way. "Ah," she said, just as Molly came in the room.

"I was just asking Mum," I told her, pointedly, "where Wupert is going to sleep."

Molly gave a snigger at the Wupert bit, but Mum didn't seem to notice.

"Well, obviously there'll have to be some changes," she began to hedge.

"Yeah, such as?" I prompted. She looked flustered, but I didn't see why I should let her off the hook. After all, she didn't have to marry Geoffrey, did she? (Or did she? Perhaps she was pregnant? No, that thought was just too horrible to contemplate…)

Mum took a deep breath. "You two girls will have to share. But I know that won't be a problem," she hurried on, waving her hands around with a jangle of bracelets, "as you two get on so well together. In fact Geoffrey was only saying the other—"

"So who's got to move out?" I interrupted.

"Well, Molly, I suppose."

"*What?*" Molly gave a roar of outrage. "Why me? It's not fair!"

"Because," Mum explained, patiently, "Mattie has the larger room. It makes sense for you both to be in there."

"No it doesn't!" Molly howled. "I've spent ages getting my room just as I want it, and now you're saying I've got to give it up!"

On she bleated, on and on, while Mum listened and nodded understandingly, and put in the odd soothing comment. I didn't know what Molly's problem was: her room resembles nothing so much as the tail end of a New Age travellers' car-boot sale, with every surface crammed with tacky ornaments or candles or joss-stick holders, no curtains (so she can see the stars), and deeply horrid bits of batik pinned to the walls. Inheriting both Mum's arty-farty sensibilities and her terminal untidiness, she uses the floor as a wardrobe and only ever makes her bed when she changes the sheets. My room, on the other hand, with its pale grey walls, charcoal carpet and bare essentials of furniture, is a masterpiece of monochromatic minimalism (or at least, compared to Molly's pit it is, but a junk shop would be minimalist compared to that). It struck me that I was definitely getting the worse side of the deal.

"If you're moving in with me," I told Molly, "I don't want any of that batik crap on my walls."

So off she went again, moan moan moan, until Mum got as near to being cross as she ever gets and told us to try to pull together instead of bickering.

"And as the eldest," she said, turning to me, "it really would be helpful if you would set an example by being sensible, Mattie, instead of winding your sister up."

So it was all my fault. Fabulous. I wanted to throw a strop too, to say it wasn't fair, that sharing a bedroom with your twelve-year-old sister sucked, and that as far as I was concerned Rupert could sleep on the sofa downstairs. But

I didn't. I maintained a quiet dignity and went calmly up to my room, thinking as I did so that Mum marrying Geoffrey was already beginning to be a big pain in the bum, and the wedding was still two months away.

The only bright spot on the horizon was the thought of Jaz's party. Rather to my surprise her dad had agreed to it, and had even booked the local village hall for the venue. It wasn't exactly Ministry of Sound, but as Jaz pointed out, it was a lot better than having it in her front room with her mum and dad breathing down our necks.

"Who d'you think I should invite?" she asked me one lunchtime. We were sitting out on the school playing field with our shirt sleeves rolled up, our ties off and our top buttons undone, attempting to get some sun on our bodies.

"Oh, I dunno — the usual crowd," I replied, vaguely. I was trying to catch glimpses of Sam Barker — who was kicking a ball around in a desultory fashion with his mates, a few metres away — without appearing too obvious.

Jaz followed my line of vision and grinned. "Yeah, he's a babe, isn't he? Don't worry, he's top of my list."

"Who?" I looked around the field in an

attempt at nonchalance. "Oh, you mean Sam? He's OK, I suppose. If you like that sort of thing."

Jaz snorted scornfully down her nose. "Yeah, like you don't!"

At that moment, Sam, aware he had an audience, started doing flashy moves with the football, kicking it from foot to foot, off his thighs and on to his head. Then he flashed a grin at us over his shoulder before shooting the ball past the lad who, acting as goalie, was standing motionless between two piles of sweatshirts dumped on the dusty grass. To my horror, Jaz applauded, and then stuck her two little fingers in the corners of her mouth and wolf-whistled.

"Shut up!" I whispered, mortified, as the bell for afternoon lessons trilled merrily in the distance.

Sam picked up his sweatshirt from the pile, slung it round his shoulders, and came towards us, carrying the football. Jaz dug me in the ribs with her elbow.

"Look, look! He's coming over! This is your big chance!" she hissed.

"My big chance for what?" I hissed back, wishing there was a convenient bush I could hide behind or, better still, a convenient lake I could shove my so-called friend into.

"To impress him with your razor-sharp wit

and incisive comments," she murmured out of the side of her mouth, as Sam drew closer.

Yeah, right, I thought. *Like he's going to take any notice of me while you're around*. Jaz has the same effect on lads as Sam has on girls. She's seriously gorgeous, with skin like burnished copper, glossy black hair, a figure to die for (despite not eating enough fresh veg), and big brown eyes like melting chocolate drops. OK, not the most romantic of images, maybe, but you get the picture. If I was a lad I'd fancy her myself.

Sure enough, it was Jaz Sam was looking at as he came sauntering across the field.

" 'Lo, girls," he said, and grinned. My stomach did a backflip; there should be a law against being that good-looking. I felt my tongue cleave to the roof of my mouth as if glued there, making any comment impossible, let alone ones of the smart-alec nature Jaz seemed to expect.

Jaz, however, had no such problem. "Hiya Sam," she trilled. "Didn't know you were so good at football."

"Well he ought to be, seeing as he's captain of the Under Seventeens," came a dry voice behind him. It was Andy Cooper, one of Sam's mates.

Jaz included him in the full 120-watt brightness of her smile. "Hello Andy!"

"Goodbye Andy." Sam tossed him the ball. "Be a mate and take this in for us, will you? I'll be along in a mo."

Andy smiled an unpleasantly knowing smile and trudged obediently off in the direction of the sports hall, while Sam hunkered down in front of us. "Jasmilla, isn't it?" he said. "And, er, Maxie?"

"Mattie," Jaz corrected him, firmly. "Listen, d'you want to come to my party?"

I could have killed her. She'd clearly never heard of the word subtlety.

It took Sam by surprise, too. He swayed back slightly on his heels and then, catching sight of Jaz's smooth brown cleavage which was shown off to great advantage by her unbuttoned white shirt, recovered enough to shuffle closer.

"Well, er, hey, that sounds, er, cool. When is it?"

"The twenty-first. The Saturday after the end of term," she explained.

Sam craned his neck to take a better look and then, realizing I was watching him, stood up suddenly and ran a casual hand through his hair. *Ran a casual, suntanned, artistically long-fingered hand through his sexily tousled tortoiseshell hair…*

"You OK?"

I realized he was looking at me oddly.

Possibly just as oddly as I'd been looking at him. I gave myself a shake.

"Fine," I croaked.

"That OK then?" Jaz persisted.

"What?"

"The party. On the twenty-first."

"Right. Yeah, cool."

"I'm bringing the invites to school next week."

"I'm not here next week."

Why not? Where are you going? Not leaving? Not — not emigrating? Not going somewhere I'll never be able to see you again?

"Why not?" Jaz quizzed him, rather forcefully I thought.

"GCSEs are over. I'm only here now because of the tennis match this afternoon."

"Oh, right." Jaz lowered her eyelids playfully. "Bet you look great in shorts."

God! Was there no end to her shamelessness? I'd sooner have died than come out with a line like that, to Sam Barker of all people — it was like chatting up Casanova.

"I do, as it happens." Sam crouched down again. "Why don't you come and watch?" he said, softly.

"We've got double Art," I blurted out, instantly regretting it as I felt the blush sweep up my neck like a hot red tide.

They both ignored me.

"I'll have to post your invitation, then," Jaz declared. "You'd better give me your address."

She dug around in her bag for a pen and he wrote his address on her hand, bending over it like some latter-day continental courtier, while I admired the square line of his jaw and the way the hair curled down the nape of his brown neck, and wished it was my hand he was writing on.

Then he was gone, with an airy wave of his hand, off to his tennis match. Jaz replaced the lid on her pen with a satisfied snap, and pushed it into her bag.

"There you go," she told me, "don't say I never do anything for you. He's coming to the party, *and* I've got his address for you. And his phone number," she added, peering at her hand.

"It's you he fancies," I said, peevishly. "He was looking down your front during your entire conversation."

"He's a boy, isn't he." She shrugged, uncaring, watching his retreating back view. "Cute butt, though."

chapter four

Rupert's school broke up for summer earlier than ours, and we suddenly started seeing a lot more of him. Every time Geoffrey came round he'd bring Rupert with him, and with the wedding getting ever closer and what seemed like interminable arrangements for him and Mum to make, the Hortons seemed to be taking up premature residency in the cottage.

I don't know exactly what it was about Rupert that set my teeth on edge. Well, I do: his appearance, the way he looked, although if you were to be mature and charitable about it you could say it wasn't his fault. He was thirteen – what thirteen-year-old boy, with no mum and no sisters to advise him and a dad with all the sartorial elegance of an Oxfam reject, could possibly have a clue about that sort of thing? But yeah, I know; I was neither mature nor charitable about him. I know that. I hate it about myself, now, in retrospect.

But there was more to it than just his appearance. He had this way of looking at us all, a kind of smug narrowing of his eyes, a tiny patronizing inscrutable smile playing around his lips, that made me want to take him by the scrawny little neck and shake him until his teeth rattled and his eyes popped… (See? Nothing very mature or charitable about that.) It was as if there was a great big cartoon thought bubble protruding from his head, and in that bubble, in enormous black letters half a metre high, were the words: I AM A THOUSAND TIMES BETTER THAN YOU, AND I CANNOT FOR THE LIFE OF ME UNDERSTAND WHY MY FATHER SHOULD WANT TO ASSOCIATE WITH SUCH A RABBLE.

It wasn't only me who felt it. Molly latched on to it too.

"Why does he think he's better than us?" she demanded one evening, after they'd left.

"Who, darling?" Mum was wafting around with two empty wine glasses and a dippy smile on her face.

"Wupert."

Mum frowned slightly at that, a tiny crease between her eyebrows, but didn't comment. "He doesn't. I'm sure he doesn't, Molly – what on earth makes you say that?"

"The way he looks at us: down his nose. He looks so…"

"Superior," I finished, helpfully.

Mum turned to me, her brow quilted with perplexity. "Oh, no, I'm sure he doesn't. You

41

must be mistaken. He seems such a nice boy. He's probably just shy."

"Shy!" I snorted disdainfully. "Wupert's not shy, unless it's shy of catching something nasty off us."

"I'm sure you're exaggerating. And don't call him Wupert, darling – it's unkind to make fun of him."

"Mustn't mock the afflicted," I muttered.

I suppose I was slightly peeved that she hadn't picked up on his air of condescension, his patronizing little smile, but the truth was, she'd have been oblivious if he'd been making wax effigies of us all to stick pins in. It was clear she was too bound up with Lover-Boy and the impending wedding to notice what was going on under her nose.

Which made it all the more surprising when she got all antsy about Jaz's party. I was on the phone to Jaz, discussing clothes and guest lists and other areas of similar importance, and when I finished Mum was standing there beside me, looking faintly anxious.

"About this party," she began, and my heart sank. As mums go she's usually pretty cool about most things, but she occasionally gets a bee in her bonnet about fairly minor details. From the look on her face, I had the feeling this was about to be one of those occasions.

"What about it?"

"How are you intending to get there; and back home, come to that?"

I waved an airy hand. "Not a problem. It's sorted." This tactic had worked well in the past. Today, however, was destined to be different.

"When you say sorted, what do you mean, exactly?"

"I'm sure I can get a lift from someone."

"Someone like...?"

"Surjit?" I suggested hopefully. Jaz's brother is just eighteen, passed his test (contrary to all expectations) six months ago, and drives a clapped-out old Ford Escort with a hole in the silencer and a registration number not of this decade, if you get my meaning. Possibly not the choice of driver most likely to put worried mothers' minds at rest.

"Not a chance," my worried mother responded, heatedly.

"Why not?" I said, equally heatedly. "Jesus, Mum, you're so biased. Just because he's not forty-something years old and doesn't drive a Volvo, you think he's unsafe on the roads."

"You bet your life I do — an opinion I share with the lads he drove around the lanes at eighty-five miles an hour, I shouldn't wonder. Though how he got eighty-five out of that heap beats me."

Hell. How did she find out about that? It was supposed to be a secret – she must have overheard me on the phone to Jaz.

"Ah," I said, sheepishly.

"How about if this forty-something Volvo driver offered her a lift?" Geoffrey said mildly, coming into the hall.

Mum turned to him. "Would you? That would be so kind. I have these terrible nightmares about her wandering along at two in the morning with her thumb stuck out, and found in a ditch twenty-four hours later with her throat cut and her toes turned up."

"Teenagers and their parties can be such a worry," Geoffrey agreed.

"Hello?" I put in, crossly. "Am I invisible, or something? And how about that time you told me about when you hitched to Glastonbury?"

"That was different," said Mum.

What a surprise. "Yeah, right."

"It was: I was nineteen, you're only fifteen."

"Four years' difference – big deal," I muttered. I was still smarting about them discussing me as if I wasn't there. No, cancel that. I'm used to being discussed as if I'm not there: isn't everyone with parents? What got me was Rupert, leaning against the door jamb and earwigging, smug smile in place, enjoying the spectacle of me being treated like a little kid.

So it was arranged that Geoffrey would take me and bring me back. I was grateful: I wouldn't hitch, despite what Mum might think, and finding transport to see my mates, most of whom live in town, six kilometres away, is a continual pain. There was, however, a price to pay. Isn't there always?

"I've been thinking," said Mum, two days before the party.

"Oh yes," I replied. I'm always suspicious when she begins sentences like that, it usually means I'm not going to like what comes next.

"It is very kind of Geoffrey to offer to give you a lift to this party."

"It is, yeah. I did thank him," I pointed out.

"And to bring you home again."

"Mmm. Look, Mum, what're you getting at?"

She gave a little sigh, and composed her features. "Rupert isn't going to know many people when he starts at St Mark's in September."

"Well, no: you don't, when you start at a new school, do you?"

"And it would be nice if he could make some friends before then, wouldn't it?"

"Would it?" I stared at her, puzzled. Then the penny started to drop. "This hasn't got anything to do with Jaz's party, has it?"

There was a silence, the kind that's known as

a pregnant pause. Then Mum began speaking very fast, as if the sheer barrage of words would stun me into submission.

"I'm sure Jaz wouldn't mind — you could introduce him to your friends — he'd enjoy himself — Geoffrey would be so grateful, I know he's anxious about Rupert fitting in — you'd both have a good time, I know you would — he'd…"

"Mum!" Molly screeched, appalled. "You're not serious! Mattie can't take old Metal Mouth to Jaz's party!"

Mum stopped, cut off in mid-stream. "Don't call him that, Molly. He can't help wearing braces." She turned to me, beseechingly. "What do you think, Mat? I wouldn't normally ask you to have someone tagging along with you and your friends, but under the circumstances…" She tailed off.

I was speechless. Well, almost. "I can't — I mean, it's just — they'll all think I'm—" I spluttered. "No way. Just, no way!"

"But why not? I'm sure Jaz would understand, if you explained. She's a sensitive girl."

"Yeah, and so'm I! Sensitive to having to babysit a — a *nerd*!"

Mum's face fell, and an expression of hurt disappointment passed across it. "Mattie, you can be very cruel. Think what that poor child's been through: his whole life's been turned upside down, it's about to change yet again, and all you can think about is the way he looks."

Put like that, she did have a point – of course she did – but there was more to it than that. It was his superior air I couldn't stomach, that way he had of looking at us as if observing some exotic and amusing creatures at a zoo. But Mum apparently hadn't noticed all that, and I didn't like being thought of as cruel, as only judging by appearances. I'm not that superficial. I could feel my defences crumbling.

"I'll think about it," I said, grudgingly.

I did think about it, but the thought didn't hold any more appeal. I even tried pointing out that, as Rupert was two years younger than me, he was hardly going to benefit from meeting my friends before starting at St Mark's. But Mum just told me that, being clever (that word again) he was only going to be one year below me, and having some familiar faces there would be better than knowing nobody.

I couldn't bear Mum's wounded, you're-letting-me-down expression. True, I couldn't bear the thought of toting Rupert to the Party of the Year, either, but I had to live with Mum's face long after the party was over. I gave in, as she and I both knew I would.

"It's cool," Jaz told me breezily, when I rang to break the bad news. "Once you're here you don't have to spend the whole evening minding him, do you? Let him fend for himself. You can still have fun."

Of course, it didn't work out like that. Things never seem to happen the way I want them to.

The evening began badly.

"Shouldn't you be getting changed?" Mum said, as I came downstairs. "Geoffrey and Rupert will be here soon."

"I am changed," I said. "This is what I'm wearing."

Mum looked at me, at my camouflage combats and eight-hole DMs, and at that moment the doorbell went.

"I'll get it," I said, hoping to avoid the comment I could see hovering around Mum's lips, but no such luck. She said it anyway, once they were indoors and grouped behind me in the sitting-room doorway, forming a little audience to her comments.

"They're not really party clothes, are they? Why don't you go up and look in my wardrobe for a nice dress?"

"I'm fine," I muttered, praying she'd just shut up.

No chance. On she rattled: "You could borrow that blue velvet one if you like – with the bits of mirror on it. You said you liked that one, didn't you?"

"On you," I growled, through gritted teeth. "It's not really me, is it?"

"Of course it is, darling!" She laughed, an irritating tinkly sound that went right through me. I'd never noticed before just what a little-girly laugh my mother has. "It would really suit you. You teenage girls are so funny! You live in trousers; you must forget what your legs look like. Don't you think she looks a bit informal for a party?"

She turned to Geoffrey, appealing to him to back her up, which thankfully he had the good sense not to do. He just smiled non-committally, and said nothing; he'd probably been taking advice, been to the library for a book on How To Get On With Your Future Stepfamily, or some such (Rule No. 1: Never Criticize).

Rupert, however, clearly possessed no such reading matter. "She does wather," he said, in his irritatingly clear prep-school voice. "More like she's going out on army manoeuvres."

I turned to him furiously, ready to rip him to shreds over his choice of party-wear, but to my surprise he actually looked reasonable for once, in stone-coloured chinos and an OK-ish green T-shirt. I hadn't even noticed his clothes when I'd opened the door.

Mum saw my head turn in his direction and misinterpreted the movement. "Don't you think Rupert looks smart? We chose those clothes together, didn't we, Rupert?"

There was no mistaking the pride in her voice, the relief that this poor motherless boy was turning to her for clothes advice, a clear sign (in her eyes) that he was accepting her as a replacement parent. I didn't have the heart to cause a scene: not then. All that came later.

Instead I summoned all my will power and turned the fury on my face into my best withering look.

"Yeah," I said. "Very hip. He's bound to pull, dressed like that," and had the immense satisfaction of watching his face turn a fetching shade of scarlet.

chapter five

With a start like that, the rest of the evening couldn't possibly go according to plan. My plan that is, which was, roughly, getting off with Sam. There were other features too, such as everyone turning to look admiringly at me as I made my entrance (solo, and definitely unencumbered by the Stepbrother-To-Be from Hell), and loads of other lads thronging round me all evening until Sam, intrigued by this mysterious and seriously sexy *femme fatale*, couldn't resist me any longer.

Ho hum. That'll teach me to fantasize. The reality, needless to say, was somewhat different.

Because of the altercations with Mum about clothes, the party had already begun when I arrived. We, I should say; when *we* arrived. I had been hoping I might be able to stride in well ahead of Rupert, greeting my friends as I went and thoroughly disassociating myself from him, but no such luck. I strode, he scuttled along behind as if determined to show me up.

"Looks like Mattie Fry's got a hot date."

I turned: it was Andy Cooper, and there standing behind him was — inevitably — Sam.

Luckily for me, Jaz came to the rescue. "Hiya, Mat," she said, grabbing me enthusiastically by the shoulders and doing the full "mwah mwah" air-kissing bit. "And this must be Rupert."

It was the first time they'd met: I'd managed to keep him away from my friends until then.

"Yeah," I said, grimly. "This is definitely Rupert."

Rupert looked as if he'd quite like her to air-kiss him too, preferably without the air, but she didn't oblige. Instead she shook his hand and said, loudly, "I hear you're going to be Mattie's stepbrother soon."

"Yes," he said unemotionally, and blinked. It made him look curiously lizard-like. "My father's going to mawwy her mother."

I glanced over at Andy and Sam to see if they'd overheard, taken in the true nature of my relationship with this *person*: Andy was eavesdropping shamelessly, but Sam had lost interest, his eyes scanning the room in a practised way to see what talent had arrived.

Still holding Rupert's hand, Jaz bore him across the hall. "There's someone over here you just must meet," she gushed, in her best hostess-with-the-mostest tones. "You'll be in his class at St Mark's when you come in September."

I waited for her by the buffet table, picking at the food.

"What d'you think?" I asked her when she came back over, having successfully delivered her package. "Isn't he the pits?" I popped a mini scotch egg into my mouth.

Jaz shrugged. "Seemed OK to me. He's very polite – he thanked me for letting him come. I thought he was quite sweet, actually."

"*Sweet?*" I stared at my friend. "We are talking about Tin Grin, aren't we? He's a total dweeb."

"Yeah, I guess the hair and the specs and the braces are a bit off-putting. But his clothes are OK – I was half expecting school uniform, after what you'd told me."

"That was Mum." I picked up a sausage roll and bit into it. "She helped him choose what to wear, apparently. Like he's a toddler or something. Who did you introduce him to?"

"Michael Stewart. My next-door neighbour. Surjit's majorly matey with his big brother. Michael's a nice kid, I thought he wouldn't mind looking after Rupert."

"Lucky old Michael." I stretched across the table for a chicken drumstick, and Jaz slapped at my hand.

"Leave the food alone, you! It's supposed to be for later."

"I thought you were supposed to be

53

vegetarian." Andy was still standing there, idly watching Sam, who by now was wrapped around a short blonde girl with a dramatically over-developed chest.

"Mum is, not me. I can't be doing with all this beansprouts-and-tofu nonsense – I grab all the meat I can get my hands on, me."

"Bit like Sam," Andy observed, drily, and Jaz made an amused snorty noise down her nose.

I leapt to Sam's defence immediately, heaven knows why. Instinct, I suppose.

"That's not true," I said, hotly. "And I don't think that girl would be very chuffed at being referred to as meat. Talk about sexist comments!"

Andy just shrugged. "It's true, though. About Sam, I mean. He's your original boob man – he thinks of girls just as bodies with interesting wobbly bits."

That put me out of the running, then. My chest famously resembles two fried eggs. "Whereas you're only interested in their minds, I suppose?" I said, sarcastically, to cover my disappointment.

Andy gave me an odd, appraising look. "I just happen to think there's more to people than what they look like, that's all," he said, and walked off.

"What did I say?" I turned to Jaz. "What's his problem?"

"Don't take any notice. It's only Andy, remember – Pillock of Year Eleven?"

Pillock of Year Eleven he might be, but I wasn't sure how smart it was to offend the best mate of the object of my desire. I had visions of them, whispering together in the loos: "You'll never guess what she said!" "No, really? What a cow!" (Did boys whisper together in loos, like girls do? I had no idea.) He might even tell Sam that the boob-man comment had been mine. That would be it: any chance I might possibly have had ruined for ever. I felt like running after Andy and apologizing, offering to fetch him some food, to dance with him, to kiss his feet – anything, so long as he put in a good word for me with Sam.

"Cheer up," Jaz told me. "Don't look so gloomy. It's my party, remember – enjoy yourself!" she commanded airily over her shoulder, as yet another of her panting admirers bore her off to dance.

It was all very well for Jaz, I thought grumpily. She didn't know what it was like to hanker after anybody: she only had to give a boy one of her come-hither looks from under her ridiculously long and luxuriant eyelashes and he'd be joining the queue of lads signing up to be her life-long slave. She has Sex Appeal. I, on the other hand, have Sacks Appeal (I only attract sad sacks), and if I try glancing up from under my eyelashes I look like a cross-eyed mental defective.

Reflecting on the unfairness of life, I lurked moodily by the food table for most of the evening, chatting in a desultory fashion to the odd passer-by and watching the rest of Jaz's guests having fun. It was a good party, I could see that, but it was no use: I absolutely wasn't in party mood. Even old Tin Grin seemed to be having a better time than me. He and Michael appeared to be getting on OK, which was, I conceded grudgingly, infinitely better than having him hanging around me all evening. I watched them exchanging nudges, daring each other to get up on the dance floor. Michael was first up, standing there twitching in that self-conscious, unrhythmic way that kids think is dancing.

Then, rather to my surprise, Rupert got to his feet. I was expecting more of the same, another demonstration from the Michael Stewart School of Dancing. I was wrong. Rupert launched himself into the air like a Harrier jump jet at take-off, limbs thrashing wildly, head lolling crazily back and forth. He looked like a scarecrow having electroconvulsive therapy. It wouldn't have been quite so bad if the music he was convulsing to had been one of those punk bands from the seventies, but it wasn't: it was a slow, smoochy number. He looked preposterous. Everyone turned to stare at him. I was totally mortified: he couldn't have embarrassed me more if he'd asked me to dance and wrapped himself round me (in much the same way Sam was now wrapped around yet another large-chested girl, as part of my brain noted idly).

I couldn't cope. I scurried off to the sanctuary of the Ladies, where I locked myself in a cubicle. What a great party this was turning out to be. I looked at my watch – only ten o'clock. Geoffrey wasn't coming to collect us until eleven. I recalled the conversation I'd had with Mum earlier on, when I was hanging out for a pick-up time of midnight, and she was suggesting ten "because of Rupert".

"He's not a baby," I'd pleaded. "Or does he turn into a pumpkin when the clock strikes twelve?"

We'd eventually compromised on eleven, with me thinking that, if Geoffrey waited outside in the car, I could possibly stretch it out for half an hour. Now I wished I'd agreed to the earlier time. All I wanted to do was go home: I thought longingly of my bed, a cup of cocoa and the luxury of confiding in my diary. *God*, I thought, *this is what it must be like to be middle-aged. How depressing*.

It was no good. I couldn't stay locked in a toilet all evening – that would be too pathetic for words. I flushed the loo, just so nobody listening would suspect I'd been hiding in there. Then I opened the cubicle door, washed my hands, fished out my lip balm from the pocket of my combats and re-applied it, fluffed up my hair in the mirror, and marched out to rejoin the party. *Go get 'em, girl!* I urged myself. *Just go out there and find somebody to dance with*. Unfortunately, my new composure was dented slightly when my trouser pocket caught on the door handle of the Ladies as I was going out. There was an ominous ripping sound.

"Oops," I said, turning to inspect the damage. "Girls just can't help tearing their clothes off when they see me."

I flew around, and my eyes met Sam's. I felt the old familiar red tide of blood as it coursed its way up my neck and face, and prayed it was too dark for Sam to notice. *Staycoolstaycoolstaycoolstaycool*...

"Oh, hi Sam," I said, casually. (*Squeaked. Nervously*.) I cleared my throat. "I didn't see you standing there. D'you often lurk outside the Ladies?"

Hell! What did I say that for? Now he'll think I'm accusing him of being a pervert!

But Sam didn't seem to have taken offence, or even, possibly, to have heard. He took me by the elbow and steered me on to the dance floor, where yet another smoochy number was playing. At least Rupert had stopped springing around like a demented frog – I could see him and Michael at the buffet, loading food on to their plates like they were preparing for a siege.

"I've been wanting to dance with you all evening," Sam purred in my ear.

"You have?" My voice disappeared up into the stratosphere. He could have fooled me; he'd barely looked in my direction up until then.

"Mm-hmm." He put his arms around me and drew me closer. I felt myself go rigid with shock. *Omigod! Sam Barker is dancing with me! What do I do?* My feet wouldn't move, they seemed to be rooted to the spot.

"Relax," he whispered. "Just relax and enjoy it." He lifted my arms and put them round his neck, and before I knew it we were pressed against each other, swaying gently in time with the music.

I dropped my head on to his shoulder and closed my eyes, hardly daring to believe this was happening, yet determined to savour the moment and store up every tiny little detail to record later in my diary, for me to pore over again and again in the future. *The feel of him, the smell, the feel of his hard muscular shoulders beneath my hands, the smell of his aftershave, the music, the music, the feel of his hands on me on my back, my waist, my bum*... ahem. I changed position slightly, shifting his hands back up towards my waist, and as I did so I felt a tap on my shoulder. I turned my head. Rupert was standing there behind me.

"Go away," I murmured. "I'm busy." I lowered my head to Sam's shoulder again. *Musky aftershave mmm nice*... Another tap, sharper this time.

"I said, go *away!*" I hissed, crossly, glancing at my watch. "It's only quarter to eleven, there's no way your dad's here yet."

"He's not." Still he stood there, gormlessly, spoiling my dance, my once-in-a-lifetime experience of being groped by Sam Barker.

"What, then? If you think I'm going to dance with you..."

Rupert opened his mouth to speak, and as he did so the music stopped so that his words rang out into the silence that followed and the entire room heard what he said.

"I don't want to dance," he said, conversationally. "You've wipped your twousers all acwoss the back, and your knickers are showing."

chapter six

REASONS FOR KILLING RUPERT:

1) He is completely insensitive
2) He enjoys showing people up in public
3) He is a total embarrassment
4) He can't dance to save his life
5) He has no dress sense whatsoever (unless helped by an adult)
6) He has a superiority complex
7) He has an irritating voice
8) He's getting zits (HA HA HA)
9) He's a specky four-eyed metal-mouthed dwarf…
10) …and a smug little git to boot
11) He's a psychotic axe-murderer
12) He farts in public
13) and picks his nose ditto
14) and wets his bed
15) He smells

I was well aware that items 7) to 15) were either not his fault, not true, or simply me being immature, but I didn't care. Just writing them in my diary made me feel better. I looked at number 15, "He smells", sitting there childishly at the bottom of the list, and added "...like a fishing smack". That seemed to fit with wetting the bed, and it had a nice sense of poetry about it.

The truth was, I hadn't felt so embarrassed since the first day of Year Eight, when Brad Smythe had gleefully announced to the entire class that I was wearing a bra (odd how often my moments of public humiliation feature underwear).

"Don't worry about it," Jaz told me over the phone the next morning. "Nobody noticed. Honestly."

"What, you mean you went round asking them?" I snarled, far from reassured.

"Course not. Really, Mat – it was too dark to see anything."

"They still heard what he said, though. They still *knew* my pants were showing, even if they couldn't actually see them."

"No they didn't."

"Yes they did. *You* heard," I accused her.

"Only 'cos I was standing next to you. Anyway, ripped trousers are really funky at the moment. Honestly, Mattie, you shouldn't worry about it. And it was only a tiny tear," she added, loyally.

It wasn't. It was massive. Practically right across the top of the leg, under the rear pocket.

I couldn't help wondering if Sam had noticed, given where he'd had his hands. Perhaps he'd even put his hand *inside*...

I shook my head to clear away the thought, which was too awful to contemplate. What if he'd thought I'd ripped them on purpose, to give him the come-on? *Oh God!*

There was a knock at the door, and Mum came in.

"You're very quiet this morning," she said. "Are you feeling all right?"

"Fine," I muttered.

"How was the party? Only you disappeared up to bed so fast when you got in, I didn't have the chance to ask."

"Oh, it was just fab."

The irony was lost on her. She glanced over to the wardrobe where my trousers were hanging over the door, the huge tear perfectly visible. Heaven knows why I'd bothered hanging them up: I may as well just have slung them out, for all the use they were going to be now. The sight of them just served to remind me of what a lousy time I'd had, how all my romantic hopes and dreams now lay in ashes at my feet (good phrase: I'd have to remember that later, for my diary).

"Oh dear," said Mum, concerned. "What happened to your trousers?"

"They got ripped," I said, dully. "As you can see."

"Oh Mattie, what a shame. I suppose I could try and mend them for you."

I saw her eyes move down to the bed where my diary lay in front of her, upside down but open at the page headed REASONS FOR KILLING RUPERT. I closed it hastily, and Mum sat down on the bed beside me, her bundle of silken skirts rustling noisily.

"Rupert seemed to enjoy the party," she said. "He was full of it when he came back, he said he'd made friends with someone called Michael."

"Good for Rupert," I muttered.

Mum put a hand over mine. "Darling, what is it? What's the matter? Do you want to talk about it?"

I considered it: I seriously did. Once upon a time, not so very long ago, Mum was the first person I told about everything, my number one confidante. But things had changed. Mum was now far too wrapped up in her wedding plans and her new man to want to be bothered by my little problems, and besides, it was no use moaning to her about Rupert. She'd made it quite plain that she didn't share Moll's and my feelings about him: complain about him, and she'd stick up for him, remind us what a hard time he'd had and how we should be making an effort to get along with him. Anyway, confiding in Mummy was for kids. I didn't need it any more. I had my friends, my diary – myself, for heaven's sake. It was time I learnt to sort out my own problems.

"Not really," I said. "I'm just a bit tired, that's all." *Tired of Rupert*...

"That'll be your Saturn influence, it's quite strong at the moment. Plus Mercury's retrograde – that always gives you a hard time."

"Yeah, yeah, Mum: whatever." Didn't she know by now I don't believe in all that astrology crap?

She stood up, an expression of gentle concern on her face, and patted my leg. "Don't sit up here by yourself all day, darling. Geoffrey's coming over later, with Rupert: it's such a lovely day, I thought you and Molly might like to show him the cove, go swimming perhaps?"

I'd sooner stick pins in my eyes. "Maybe."

"Why don't you come downstairs now? I'll make you a nice cup of camomile tea."

"Mum," I said, with a heavy sigh, "there are some things in life that just can't be cured with camomile tea."

When we first came to live at Brandy Bay we thought we'd come to Paradise, Moll and me – as I think I've already said. Well, any child

65

would, especially ones like us, coming as we did from our urban, inner-city life to the little lime-kiln worker's cottage with its own private and secluded cove.

That's what we thought, anyway. It was November when we moved in, cold and damp and storm-lashed as only north-facing British coastlines can be in the winter; isolated and desolate and inhospitable, two kilometres to the nearest shop and almost four to the nearest neighbours, and we'd never been so happy. It was the isolation that did it: just the three of us, tucked up together away from the shouting and the fights and the drunken violence that had constituted our family life up till then.

That first Christmas was the best I can remember. There were few presents and even fewer frills and luxuries, but Mum decorated the cottage with candles, the plain white house-hold variety stuck on saucers, and we festooned the place with holly and ivy that we'd collected from the woods that go right down to the edge of the cove. We toasted each other with apple juice as we ate our Christmas dinner of cauli-flower cheese and home-made mince pies, and basked in the unfamiliar luxury of peace and quiet.

It was an illusion, of course, the isolation and tranquillity. The spring soon arrived, bringing primroses that studded the wooded banks down to the bay and later, bluebells and a soft new greening of the trees: and the tourists. We should have guessed – or Mum should have – that the prospect of a deserted Devon cove would be irresistible to holidaymakers, even one with a walk of over a kilometre from the nearest car park (although the walk back, uphill, meant we rarely saw the same faces twice).

All through the spring and the summer they came, the tourists – attracted by the small and perfectly formed (if rather stony) beach, with its sweep of wooded hillside, its natural rock pools, its waterfall and disused limekiln and colourful, romantic history of smugglers. They brought with them their dogs and their hordes of screaming excited children, their picnics, shrimping nets, rubber rings, armbands and lilos, and all the other assorted essential detritus of days out at the seaside. A lot of which they left behind, needless to say: sometimes thrilling things (to a ten year old) like an abandoned Barbie, or a forgotten disposable camera with a few shots of film left, but mostly empty Coke or beer cans, screwed-up cling film from sand- wiches, black and slimy banana skins, discarded pasty wrappers or cigarette packets.

Mum always made Moll and me go around

with a black bin-liner after they'd all gone, collecting up all the rubbish. We'd moan like hell as we did it, slipping around on the rocks in our jelly shoes and cursing the holidaymakers, but we still did it. We refuse point blank, these days. Let them take their own garbage home, we rage, but of course they don't. Mum does it now, out of respect for the environment, the goodness of her heart, or just because she's a soft touch – who knows.

It spoiled those first summer months for Molly and I, the fact that what we'd considered our private cove wasn't private at all. We got used to it, of course: it was still heaven compared to what we'd left behind. We got used to sharing the beach with strangers, or swimming early or late to avoid them. We even got used to the continual knocks at the cottage door, asking for drinks of water or use of the loo or telephone, or even (once or twice) demanding ice lollies or cream teas. When I was about twelve I put a notice up in the front porch, a sign writ large with black marker pen on cardboard: THIS IS A PRIVATE HOUSE. IT IS NOT A CAFF. WE HAVE NO PUBLIC FACILITYS. (My spelling's improved since then.) Mum made me take it down, she said it would make the visitors think we were unfriendly. So what, I said: I *feel* unfriendly when they come trooping past, staring in the windows. But she still made me take it down.

It was strangely quiet that day, the day we showed the cove to Rupert for the first time; unusually empty for a Sunday afternoon in late July. The only reason I agreed to taking him down there was because he didn't look keen when Mum suggested it, a look of distaste on his face as he glanced down at his unsuitable, highly polished, black school-approved shoes.

"The cove?" he enquired, politely. "Why? What is there to see?"

"Well, the sea, of course," said Mum, smiling. "You could swim."

"I don't swim." Still the same polite voice, the same bland expression.

"Of course you do," said Geoffrey, rather crisply.

"I haven't got my twunks."

"They're in the car," his father said. "I bunged them in when Alice phoned and mentioned swimming. Perhaps you should leave them at the cottage now: they'll be more use to you here than at the flat for the next week or so."

Did I imagine the look that crossed Rupert's face: the slightly flared nostrils, the almost imperceptible widening of the eyes? Possibly. I suffer so much from embarrassment myself, from alarm or mortification caused by other

69

people's words or actions, that I can detect discomfort in others from fifty paces, with or without physical signs.

Rupert made a last-ditch attempt to wriggle out of it, to avoid being escorted down to the beach by these two howwid girls he was soon to share a home with.

"I'm not wearing the wight clothes," he said, with studied calm. "Or shoes," he added.

"Your shorts and deck shoes are in the car too," said Geoffrey, briskly.

If he'd been somebody else – practically any-body else – I'd have felt sorry for Rupert, shared a sense of kinship with him for having the sort of parent who chivvied you along and embarrassed you in public. But hey, come on – this was Droopy Rupey we were talking about.

"Come along then, Rupert," I said, with as much softening of the R and poshing-up of my voice as I dared in front of Mum and Geoffrey. "Get your togs on – we're going swimming."

Molly did her best as a tourist guide, showing him the waterfall and the limekiln and the big cave as proudly as if she owned them, but he wasn't interested, you could tell. He just plodded along beside her in the shorts (long flapping things, displaying his unusually large white bony knees) he'd been forced to wear, with

70

his usual supercilious expression on his face.

"Why's it called Brandy Bay?" He pronounced it Bwandy Bay. It was the only spark of interest he'd shown.

Molly turned to him, her face animated. "Smugglers," she hissed theatrically. "There were loads round here. See that cave there? That's where they used to store it all."

He narrowed his eyes. "Store all what?"

"You know." Molly waved a vague hand. "Kegs of rum and stuff."

"Bwandy for a parson, baccy for a clerk?"

I recognized the quote, heard the irony in his voice, but Molly didn't.

"Yeah. Exactly."

"Oh, sure. Smugglers!" he sneered, curling his lip with disdain.

Molly took instant offence on the cove's behalf. "There were!" she said hotly. "There were smugglers here in the nineteenth century – everyone round here knows that!"

Rupert regarded her for a long moment. "Actually," he said, smugly, "I think you'll find it was the eighteenth centuwy." He turned, and picked his way without haste over the rocks and shingle to the water's edge.

"Know-all," Molly shouted shrilly, after his retreating back. "It must be great to know everything!"

"Oh, take no notice," I advised her. "Eighteenth century, nineteenth century – what does it matter?"

"It's just the way he says things, like he's a teacher or something. And his stupid *superior* face: he really gets on my nerves."

"Mine too." But I was in no mood to discuss Rupert's more unpleasant qualities; I wanted a swim.

Moll and I just pulled off our clothes to our swimsuits underneath and dived into the water, but Rupert shilly-shallied around at the edge, changing modestly beneath a towel and then sliding gingerly in, a millimetre at a time, teeth chattering.

We were swimming in a pool formed partly naturally, by the rocks, and partly built from stone and concrete. We'd never known what it had been made for – something to do with the limeworkers, perhaps – but the water was changed naturally twice daily when the tide came in and over the sides, and when the tide went out again the pool warmed up in the sun. It was our favourite swimming place, and it was rare to have it to ourselves, as we did today.

"You're not cold, are you?" I swam up to Rupert and splashed him. "Come on in – don't be such a wuss!"

He shuddered, but otherwise ignored me. Lowering himself the final few centimetres into the tepid water, he swam off with a precise, prim little breaststroke. I pulled myself up on to a ledge and sat watching him. Without his glasses, and with his neck stretched up to keep his head out of the water, he looked like an ungainly turtle. His skinny white torso and limbs glowed with a pale ghostliness beneath the surface, giving him the appearance of a shell-less crab, or an odd marine creature that spends its life at the bottom of the ocean, away from any source of fresh air and sunlight. I was so busy watching him with a kind of fascinated disgust that I didn't realize anyone was approaching until a voice came suddenly from the rocks behind me, making me jump.

"Yo, Mattie! What you doing here?"

Startled, I spun around. It was Andy Cooper: and usually, where there was Andy Cooper, there was also…

Yup. There he was, looming round the rocks with a great big cheesy smile on his face. Sam Barker. I leapt to my feet, nearly sliding off my rocky perch as I did so, and grabbing a towel, attempted to wrap it around my lower half, sarong-style, hoping that the expression on my face resembled cool inscrutability rather than the flustered panic I felt inside.

"I live here," I managed to say. "What's your excuse?"

Sam clambered up on to the ledge beside me, and my heart hammered: I'd never before been so close to him while wearing so little. He gave me a quick, appraising glance: up and down, and then up again, as if he was a farmer at market debating whether I was worth the asking price.

"You mean you're, like, a cave-dweller?"

Woah! Sarcasm! I am definitely getting somewhere.

"No, I mean I live over there." I gestured with my head towards the cottage. I didn't dare use my hand, in case the towel-sarong fell down and exposed my flabby thighs.

At that point, Molly, who'd been lurking at the other end of the pool, swimming under-water and trying to tip Rupert up, came splashing over.

"Hiya," she said, and floated on her back. "You found us, then?"

Sam and Andy exchanged glances. I smelt conspiracy.

"What d'you mean, they found us? What's going on?" I demanded suspiciously.

"Oh, Andy was asking me at school the other day where we lived," she said, off-handedly, and swam off again.

There was an embarrassed silence, during which Sam and Andy looked at each other again.

"We've been meaning to come out here for a while," Andy said, eventually. "Then someone said you and your sister live at Brandy Bay, so I asked Molly how to get here."

"Oh, right." Why didn't I believe him? Possibly because, unlike me and Moll, they'd lived round here all their lives. Saying they didn't know how to get to Brandy Bay was like Londoners saying they didn't know where Trafalgar Square was. "How did you get here, then?"

"Bike." Andy hitched a thumb in the direction of the shore, where two battered-looking mountain bikes reclined in a heap on the shingle. "Look, I really need a swim after all that. You coming?" he asked Sam.

"In a bit." Sam sat down on the ledge, and Andy shrugged and disappeared behind a rock, presumably to get changed.

"Well," Sam said to me, and grinned suddenly.

"Well," I said back. *What repartee, what thrusting rapier-like wit…*

"God, it's hot." He sat back and peeled off his shirt, displaying his smooth brown chest and shoulders, muscled from cricket and tennis and swimming. The comparison with Rupert and his soft white unfit body was almost cruel. I swallowed.

"Well," I said again, and sat down beside him. I didn't actually mean to: my knees just kind of gave way.

Sam eyed me languidly. "Actually," he said, "there was a reason for coming over this afternoon. What you might call an anterior motive."

"Ulterior," I said, automatically. That's another bad habit I've got: correcting other people's speech.

Sam blinked. "What?"

"I said, ult— never mind. What were you going to say?"

"Well, I just wondered – you might not be keen, in which case, hey, no worries – but how about coming out with me some time?"

I stared at him for a full thirty seconds, during which time I was aware of my mouth hanging open like a lizard trying to catch insects on its tongue.

"You what?" I managed to croak.

The faintest look of impatience crossed over his face. "I said, d'you want to come out with me some time? We could go bowling, or to see a movie."

"Oh, right. Oh, yes, yes please," I began to babble. This was incredible! Sam Barker – *Sam*

Barker – was asking me out! "When? I mean, when did you have in mind?"

"Well, that's the bummer." Sam frowned and stood up, uncrossing his long legs. "I'm off on holiday with the parents tomorrow. I'm back a week on Saturday – maybe we could do something then?"

"Oh, yes – yes – that would be great – any time you like – I'm sure I'll be free then."

If you want to take me out I'll make sure my whole life's free – I'll clear my diary for ever – I'll...

"You can't."

"What?" I looked down in the direction of the voice: it was Rupert, still in the water and clinging on to the edge of the rocks by my feet. He'd clearly been eavesdropping. "What on earth d'you mean, I can't? I don't have to ask your permission to do things!"

"No," Rupert agreed mildly. "But you can't do anything a week on Saturday. It's the wedding."

The bloody wedding! Not only was my entire life destined to change after it, but the wretched thing was now threatening to sabotage my love life too. It wasn't fair, it just wasn't fair...

Sam gave a disinterested shrug. "Hey, I don't want to interrupt anything you guys have planned."

77

Anything us guys had planned? I couldn't bear it: Sam thought I was turning him down because I was doing something with Rupert!

I tried to tell him it wasn't like that, he'd got it wrong, but all I could seem to do was gabble incoherently. Luckily, Molly had overheard everything, and came over to intervene.

"Our mother's marrying his dad," she explained. Now, why couldn't I have just said that, the bare facts, without burbling on like an escapee from an asylum?

"Right," said Sam, looking at me. "Perhaps afterwards, then?"

But before I could answer, Molly cut in again. "We're going away afterwards. All of us. Mum's calling it a Stepfamily Honeymoon," she said, disgustedly, but Sam had clearly lost interest or patience or something, because he slung his Ben Sherman shirt over his bronzed shoulder and began to clamber down, back over the rocks.

"Some other time then," he said, as he went.

"I'll give you a ring, shall I, once I'm back?" I called after him, anxiously.

"No, I'll ring you."

His voice was faint as he negotiated the rocks. I watched forlornly as he and Andy — who obviously hadn't been swimming at all — collected their bikes and pushed them up the beach to the lane, where they rode off without so much as a backward glance.

"I know you fancy him," said Molly, matter-of-factly, as she hauled herself from the water and sat at my feet, "but you shouldn't fall over him like all the other girls do, you know. I've seen them. He already thinks he's God's gift, and now he'll think you're desperate. Hey, Mat, lend us your towel, will you? I've got water in my eyes."

I turned to her, hot with anger. "Get your own towel," I told her furiously. "And when I need romantic advice from a twelve year old, I'll ask you, right? Until then, do us a favour and keep your opinions to yourself!"

And I flung myself off the ledge and over the rocks towards the cottage, ignoring the little voice in my head that was telling me I shouldn't be taking my feelings out on Molly. The trouble was, part of me knew, deep down, that she was right about Sam. Not only that, but how the hell was he going to ring me when, as far as I knew, he didn't have my phone number?

chapter seven

In the end Mum and Geoffrey got married in neither church nor registry office, but in a castle about thirty kilometres' drive away. At least, they call it a castle, and I suppose once upon a time that's exactly what it was, but at some stage in the last hundred years somebody thought it would be a good idea to tack a hotel on to the side of it, and because it's in a pretty bit of Devon more people wanted to come and stay in it, and so it kept on expanding. So now it's a rather ugly collection of buildings of all shapes, sizes and colours, but because it's got the word "castle" in its name people think it's dead grand, and it's very popular for weddings. Oh well. There's no accounting for taste, or as Jaz is fond of saying, one man's meat is another man's *poisson*.

The day before the wedding it occurred to me I didn't even know where it was happening. I felt a bit bad about that – perhaps I should have taken more interest in it all, perhaps Mum would have liked my input, my thoughts on things – but the feeling of guilt didn't last long.

After all, it wasn't my wedding, was it? And if she'd wanted my help, she'd only had to ask.

Despite the castle, it was all quite low-key, with only a handful of guests and Mum floating happily around in a weird outfit that looked as if it was made out of a load of silk scarves, which was her idea of a wedding dress. Molly thought it was all fab, I could tell, even though she tried to look blasé and uninterested. She's too young to be cynical. And I couldn't help reflecting that, a couple of years ago, I'd have thought it pretty fab, too. My mum, getting married to someone who clearly thought she was wonderful. But as it was I was just overcome with the naffness of it all: Mum in her Isadora Duncan kit standing next to Geoffrey, in full morning dress (whose idea was *that*?), with Rupert as ring-bearer in a smaller version of his father's get-up. I've never seen the point of morning dress: it made the Hortons look like a couple of funeral directors.

And then the reception afterwards, where we didn't even sit down and eat properly, but had to wander round holding a plate in one hand and a glass in the other, trying to look as if we were enjoying ourselves whilst wishing for a third hand to get food to mouth. Then Mum insisted on making a speech, during which she burbled on in a New Age, champagne-fuelled way about karma and cleansed auras. Deeply embarrassing.

The only good thing was that Molly and I weren't made to be bridesmaids (although I have a sneaky suspicion that Moll would have quite liked it). However, I was forced to wear a dress – Mum loaned me one of her slightly less hippy-dippy ones – but I did manage to get away with wearing my DMs with it. I'd have worn my combats, if they hadn't been ruined. I'm not into dressing up: what's the point, if you don't feel like celebrating the event everyone else is dressed up for?

After the wedding, as promised, we all went away together to the Lake District. All of us, like some idyllic scene from *The Sound of Music*: the Von Horton Family Singers' Summer Outing. Except we didn't sing. There wasn't much to sing about, if you ask me.

If I were to be honest (rather than just crabby), I'd have to admit I'd been quite looking forward to it. I couldn't remember the last time we'd had a holiday, Mum and Molly and me, unless you counted the time we'd just left Manchester when we stayed with an old college friend of Mum's in Somerset, and that wasn't a holiday, although Mum had told us beforehand that's what it was. She went out every day looking (as I now realize) for some-where for us to live, while Moll and me were left in this woman's flat to amuse ourselves. Somerset had sounded lovely, a pastoral vision of gently rolling green hills and contentedly grazing sheep, but the bit Mum's friend lived in wasn't like that at all: it was late October, it rained non-stop, and the flat overlooked a main road along which the traffic swished relent-lessly through the rain, and beyond that a drab featureless grey beach that was nothing but mud. Mum's friend Ruby tried hard to be kind, but you could tell she wasn't used to looking after kids. Molly and I watched an awful lot of videos that fortnight, and Ruby was dead glad when the time came for us to leave; even I, at the age of ten, could hear the relief in her voice underneath her words of concern and regret.

The problem with this holiday, this com-munal honeymoon, was that it wasn't just Mum and Molly and me. Obvious, isn't it? Of course Geoffrey was going to be there – Mum had just married the guy, for heaven's sake – and where Geoffrey went, Tin Grin went too. Stands to reason, right?

Wrong. That's what I'm trying to say. Call me stupid, in denial, or whatever, but the penny just hadn't dropped. When Mum had shown me the picture of where we were going to stay, the brochure with the photograph of this whitewashed little cottage in the middle of a Cumbrian fell, I hadn't grasped the reality of the situation. The reality of sharing a bathroom with two males, of finding the loo seat up and bristles and a soapy tidemark around the sink every day after Geoffrey's morning shave. The reality of seeing their faces at the table every mealtime: supper time, lunchtime and, worst of all (I'm not at my best in the mornings), breakfast time. The reality of sharing a bed-room with Molly, and of going off to bed each evening, leaving Mum and Geoffrey alone downstairs – and knowing, just knowing, that soon they'd be climbing the stairs together to their little double bedroom under the eaves. (I forced myself to stop thinking at that point; there's only so far your imagination should take you.) The reality of all squeezing in to Geoffrey's Volvo every day to go off exploring the fells. And the reality, the continuous fact of their presence: the two extra coats hanging in the hallway, two extra (large) pairs of walking boots left lying around, two extra sets of dishes to wash up, surplus damp towels in the bath-room and empty cereal packets and milk bottles and coffee jars left lying around in the kitchen – the room they took up, those two extra bodies, the sheer physical space they occupied, five of us where before we'd only been three – it took a lot of getting used to. I'll never get used to it, I told myself, never: this is how it's going to be from now on, and I made no effort to stop myself thinking of them as strangers; foreigners, usurpers.

Even so, there were still moments of pleasure. Having lived in the middle of nowhere for the past five years Molly and I are dyed-in-the-wool country girls now, despite our early city life upbringing: we're used to walking kilometres in all weathers, enjoy it, even. Our feet are immune to blisters and our noses no longer run in the wind and rain, which I guess is ideal preparation for a holiday in the Lake District.

There was a lot of wind and rain that holiday. Mum and Geoffrey were keen to get out on the fells – Geoffrey was also used to real weather, I supposed, being an archaeologist – and Molly and I were happy to tag along. Not so Rupert, however. Every morning he made it plain he didn't want to go out walking – "can't we just stay in and play Scwabble?" he pleaded, halfway through the stay – and every day he moaned continuously as we were walking. He was cold, he was wet. His boots rubbed. His cagoule dripped on his trousers. The hills were too steep, he got out of breath going up and his legs hurt going down. He was hungry at eleven o'clock in the morning and insisted on eating his sandwiches, then he felt sick. Even the day we went up Helvellyn and the rain stopped and the sky turned blue and the sun miraculously came out and shone on the dappled surface of Thirlmere far below us, turning it to beaten pewter, he complained.

"Look," said Geoffrey, taking Rupert by the shoulders and turning him around. "Just look at that view. Isn't that something?"

"I'm all hot and sweaty," Rupert whinged. "And the sun's in my eyes. Is it lunchtime yet?"

"God," said Molly disgustedly, in my ear. "What a wuss."

After that, Molly and I stopped striding out in front, setting the pace, and began to lag behind with Rupert.

"It's kind of the girls to help Rupert along," I overheard Geoffrey say to Mum, but there was no kindness in our actions. We started sniping at him, teasing him, calling him names and mocking his unfitness; but all in undertones, of course. We didn't want Mum and Geoffrey cottoning on to what we were doing.

"Come on, Tin Grin," Molly jeered softly, watching him plod morosely up yet another hill. "Can't you go any faster than that? God, you're pathetic!"

"Put some backbone into it, Wupert, do!" I joined in. "You look so droopy."

"Droopy Rupert!"

"No, Droopy Rupey!"

"Dwoopy Wupey, Dwoopy Wupey, Dwoopy Wupey!"

We shouldn't have done it, I know, but he was such an easy target. He never fought back, never stood up for himself or told us to shut up. He just clamped his jaw shut, put his head down and stumped moodily along.

Getting a reaction from him became a challenge to us, but one day we went too far. We were walking a pace or two behind him and Molly was quietly chanting "Droopy Rupey" to the tune of the hymn with the words "Bread of Heaven" — "Droopy Rupey, Droopy Rupey, Droopy Droopy Droopy Rupe (Droopy Rupe)!" — when she changed it on the final chorus to Loopy Rupey. The effect on Rupert was dramatic. He yanked the rucksack containing his lunch off his back, and hurled it to the ground with an oddly high-pitched howl. Then he subsided on to a nearby rock and began to cry; dry-eyed, square-mouthed sobs, like a toddler.

Molly and I looked at him, nonplussed, and then at each other.

"D'you think we ought to get Mum?" I began

to say, but there was no need. Mum and Geoffrey were already charging over like the relief cavalry.

"What's the matter?" Mum asked Rupert anxiously, over and over, an arm around his heaving shoulders. "What's the matter, darling? Are you hurt? What've you done? What's the matter?"

Geoffrey turned to me, calmly. "Did you see what happened, Mattie?"

"He hasn't hurt himself," I said, with a shrug. "He just threw himself down there. He threw his lunch down, too," I added, indicating his rucksack.

At that point, Rupert stood up abruptly and pushed Mum away. It must have caught her off-balance, because she staggered backwards slightly, a shocked look on her face.

"Get off me, you bag!" he yelled. As insults go I suppose it wasn't so bad – not when you consider what he'd been putting up with from Moll and me – but it had a galvanizing effect on his father. Geoffrey strode over to him purposefully.

"Stop that at once," he commanded. He picked up Rupert's rucksack and thrust it at him. "Put this back on."

Rupert did so, snivelling. "Don't want to walk any more," he sniffed.

"I did rather gather that," his father said, drily. He turned to us. "I think I'd better take him back to the car. We'll see you back there, OK? Don't rush." Mum started to intervene, to say we'd all go back, of course we would, but Geoffrey raised an authoritarian hand. "There's absolutely no reason why you and the girls should have your day spoilt. Besides, I think it's time Rupert and I had a little chat; don't you, old son?"

Rupert glowered, and pushed at a tuft of grass with the toe of his boot, and the two of them walked slowly off down the hill towards the car park.

As soon as they were out of earshot, Molly erupted.

"God," she said, buzzing with indignant excitement. "Did you see that? Mega-tantrum, or what? How old is he for God's sake, three?"

She clucked away disapprovingly until her attention was caught by a sheep with its lamb that had wandered on to the path and were gawping curiously at us. She's a sucker for animals, is Molly, particularly baby ones.

"Oh, look!" she cooed. "What a doody little lamb!" And off she went to talk to the sheep, Rupert and his tantrum temporarily over-shadowed.

Left alone together, Mum looked at me

narrowly. "Are you sure you don't know what set Rupert off? *Something* must have upset him."

Yeah, I thought grimly, and I bet he's bending old Geoffrey's ear right now about how mean and nasty those wotten girls were being. I wasn't about to tell Mum about it, though. I mean, what was there to tell? A little bit of name-calling – big deal. Rupert was going to have to learn to stick up for himself when he was at St Mark's. Let Geoffrey fill Mum in on the details, I thought. Let him tell her how his precious son had majorly overreacted to a spot of teasing.

OK: I felt guilty. Of course I did. But I also couldn't help feeling a little tingle of satisfaction, a small fizz of pleasure that Rupert had shown himself up in such a completely childish way.

"He said you were a bag," I pointed out to Mum, ignoring her question. "And you were only trying to help. That was really uncalled-for."

She turned to me, her eyes troubled. "You did see I was trying to help, didn't you, Mat? I wasn't interfering, was I? It didn't look as if – as if I was trying to take his mother's place?"

I felt a pang of sympathy for her. "No," I said, and squeezed her arm. "You were being kind; anyone could see that."

"I am trying, Mattie. But he doesn't make it easy, sometimes. He seems to want to make me feel shut out."

I felt a spurt of pure pleasure that she was confiding in me like this, that she was at last beginning to see the other side of Rupert instead of making excuses for him all the time. I spread out my arms languorously and tilted my head back, enjoying the feel of the sun on my face. "Never mind," I said. "We've got the rest of the day to ourselves. It's just like the old days isn't it, just the three of us? Let's make the most of it."

But to my surprise, Mum shook her head. "We can't," she said. She sounded annoyed. I couldn't imagine why she was annoyed with me. It was hardly my fault. "How can we, Mattie? Things are different now, surely you know that. It's not just the three of us any more. We'll give them half an hour to cool off, then we'll go and find them."

"But why?" I burst out. I felt disappointed, cheated of some time alone together. "They obviously don't want to be with us!"

"That's not true." Mum gave a sigh and sat down on the rock where, five minutes earlier, Rupert had thrown his wobbly. "Rupert's having problems with this holiday. He's not used to all the walking, for a start; I did wonder, when Geoffrey suggested it, but he felt sure Rupert would be able to cope. He thought it would be better than having us all cooped up in the cottage together."

"Well, he was wrong, wasn't he?" I said, sullenly.

"It looks like it. And the weather hasn't helped."

"It's only a bit of rain, for Chrissakes! What's the matter with him, anyway; is he going to melt if he gets wet?"

"And actually," Mum went on, her voice dead calm and reasonable, "you haven't helped much either. You and Molly. I've heard you teasing him, both of you. It's not kind, Mattie. This stepfamily thing isn't easy, it's not easy for anyone, but you're not helping things at all."

I felt caught out, wrong-footed. What could I say? There was me, thinking Rupert had blotted his copybook by throwing a wobbly, and suddenly here it was, all my fault.

Mum looked steadily at me. I didn't like the expression on her face. I hadn't a clue what she was going to say next, but I felt sure I wasn't going to like it.

"You know," she said at last, completely changing the subject, "I was really disappointed that you didn't take more interest in the wedding."

Whatever I'd been expecting her to say next, it certainly wasn't that. I stared at her. "What d'you mean?"

"You didn't seem to want to know anything about it."

"But you didn't tell me anything! You only wanted to talk to Lover-Boy about it."

"Mattie!" Now she looked really upset. "How can you say that? I tried to talk to you about it, to include you in the plans, heaps of times, but you just brushed me aside!"

"When?" I was baffled. "When did you try to talk to me?"

"When I asked you about the ceremony, whether you thought St Petroc's or the castle would be best. When I showed you the different menu options for the reception. When I asked you about coming shopping with me for my dress. When I—"

"OK, OK," I muttered. Now she mentioned it, I did remember her showing me various things. Vaguely. It was around the time Jaz was organizing her party, and I'd been really bound up with that. And I did recall her asking me about going shopping, but I can't bear shopping with Mum, especially for clothes. She wants to go into every single shop, and try everything on about twenty times, just to make sure she's getting exactly the right thing. Anyway, she hadn't said it was for her wedding dress: I was sure she hadn't.

"But you always said you were busy," she added, sadly.

It was the sadness that did it. "Look, I'm sorry, all right?" I said. "I didn't realize you wanted my opinion that badly. You never said. You only had to say 'Mattie, I'd really like you to help me choose my dress,' and I'd have come like a shot. You know I would."

"It didn't feel like that, darling. It felt as if you weren't interested. Almost – almost as if you didn't want me to marry Geoffrey."

How could I answer her? How could I tell her that Geoffrey was OK, just about, but it was Rupert that was the great big fly in the ointment? How could I say that, in my opinion, she and Geoffrey had been fine just as they were, seeing each other a few times a week and no strings attached, without having to go through all the ridiculous palaver of weddings and wafty frocks and speeches and communal honeymoons?

Well, I couldn't, could I? And I especially couldn't tell her that, as far as I was concerned, the worst bit was yet to come; when we got back and had to share our home with them.

So I just shrugged and gritted my teeth, and came out with some blah about being sorry for not seeming to be interested, and that of course I was glad she'd married him, if that's what she wanted, and then Moll wandered over from her sheep and we had a big soppy group hug; and presently we went off down the hill together to the car park, where we found Geoffrey and Rupert restored by the magical appearance of an ice-cream van and a Ninety-Nine apiece.

chapter eight

The worst thing about getting back home was moving all Molly's things into my room, to make way for Rupert. The first night back was OK – he slept downstairs, on the sofa, and I could just pretend that everything was normal and nothing had changed – but when I woke up the next morning I couldn't kid myself any longer.

For a start, there was a socking great van parked on the lane outside the cottage. As I watched from my bedroom window, Geoffrey and Mum emerged from the back of it and staggered down the tailgate, carrying an enormous mahogany desk between them.

I shoved my feet into some slippers and rushed down the stairs and out of the open front door.

"What's going on?" I demanded. "Where on earth's *that* going to go?"

"Oh, hello Mattie," Mum greeted me, over her shoulder. "Darling, d'you think we could just put this down for a moment? My back's killing me."

"Of course." Geoffrey put his end of the desk down carefully on the concrete driveway and smiled warmly at me. "I'll just go and see what's left to come in before we go back for the next lot." He went back up the tailgate, whistling cheerfully.

"The next lot?" I repeated. "God, how much stuff's he got? And where *is* that desk going to go?"

"In the dining room." Mum pushed a strand of her hair off her forehead. She looked hot, but thoroughly happy. She beamed at me, and patted the desk as if it was an animal. "It's beautiful, isn't it?"

I shrugged. "It's OK. But I don't see how it's going to fit in the dining room, with all your stuff in there. Where are you going to work?"

"We'll manage. I don't need a lot of it any more, anyway; it's about time I had a good clear-out."

I gave a disbelieving snort. My mother and clear-outs aren't usually mentioned in the same sentence. "Yeah, right."

Geoffrey re-emerged from the back of the van. "There's just Rupe's bed and some boxes, then we're done."

"I'll leave you to it. I'm going round Jaz's today; I'll see you later, OK?"

I turned on my heel to go in, but Mum put a hand on my shoulder. "Oh no, darling, you can't do that. Not today."

"Why not?" We always go and see each other after one of us has been away: it's an unwritten convention. "I have to, Mum. I want to see what's been going on while I've been away."

"I don't expect anything very much has changed in a week." Mum pushed her hair off her face again. "I need you and Molly to sort your rooms out today, remember? We're bringing all Rupert's things over."

I tutted with annoyance. "Do I have to?"

"Of course you have to, darling. You can't leave Molly to do it all, that wouldn't be fair."

I didn't feel particularly fair; that was the problem. I looked around in an exaggerated manner. "Where's *Rupe* then? I don't see him helping."

A very faint shadow flickered across her face. "He's back at the flat, packing." Her voice was quite patient; perhaps I'd imagined the shadow. "Why don't you go in and get dressed, and have some breakfast? Then you and Molly can decide where everything's going. You never know, it might even be quite fun."

Who was she trying to kid? I stomped moodily back indoors where I discovered Molly in the shower and no cornflakes in the packet, neither of which did anything to improve my mood.

The rest of the day was spent bickering with Molly about how the room should be arranged. Her idea of sorting things out was to come in with great armfuls of her belongings and dump them on the floor, and then stir the whole mess around with her toe while humming tunelessly.

"For God's sake!" I exploded, after about two hours of this. "How are we supposed to get this lot tidied up? Why can't you be more organized?"

"I'm perfectly organized," Molly said, calmly. "I know exactly what's here."

"You can't possibly!" I stood back, hands on hips, and surveyed the boiling mass of my sister's possessions which by now was threatening to take over the entire room. "What's this – and this – and *this*, for crying out loud?" I picked up a manky piece of cloth that looked like the result of a particularly unsuccessful attempt at tie-dyeing. "You can't possibly want or need this!"

"Yes I do: give it back!"

She darted forward to snatch it from my hands, but I side-stepped her and, grabbing a black bin-liner, began pulling things from the pile at random and chucking them in.

"What are you doing?" Molly wailed. "I want all that!"

"No you don't," I said briskly. "Just chuck the whole lot out; you know it makes sense."

"Stop it!" She clutched one side of the bin-liner and pulled at it. "Stop it, Mattie! Give those back!"

"No way! It's just rubbish – I'm not having it all in my room, you've got to sort it out." I pulled the other side of the bin-liner, even harder.

"*Our* room – it's ours now, remember?" she yelled, furiously.

"How could I forget?" I yelled back, equally furiously, and we pulled and yanked at the bin-liner until the inevitable happened and it split, scattering its contents even further across the floor.

"Now look what you've done!" Molly shrieked.

"What *I've* done – I like that!" I sprang across the room and snatched up a reel of parcel tape from the chest of drawers. "Right. This is my side of the room—" I indicated it with my hand, "and this is yours. And this goes down the middle to show what's what."

I pulled at the end of the tape and stuck it on to the wall, unrolling it across the carpet and kicking Molly's things over it as I went. When I got to the doorway I tore off the end with my teeth, savagely, and banged it down on the threshold of the room with the heel of my hand.

"There! And anything of yours that I find over my line gets chucked back over. Like this," I added, picking up Moll's beloved blue stuffed rabbit and lobbing it at the wall.

Molly gave a squeal. "Flumpy! You pig, Mattie." And she picked up my diary from the bedside table and threw it at me, hard. I ducked, just in time, and it flew over my head and landed with a thud in the open doorway.

Open, but not empty; for standing there, with a bemused expression on his face, was Geoffrey.

"Ah," he said, mildly. He bent and, picking up the diary, handed it to me. "Yours, I believe."

"Yeah," I said hotly, "but I didn't chuck it at you."

"I didn't chuck it at him," Molly retorted, "I was aiming it at you!"

"That's all right then." For a moment, I thought he was going to laugh. It irritated the hell out of me: there's nothing worse than not being taken seriously when you're in the middle of a row with someone.

I strode over to him and folded my arms. "Can I help you?" I asked, loftily.

"Funny, I was going to ask you the same thing. You two have been up here slaving away for hours, and it struck me you might appreciate a helping hand."

"Oh no," I said, with heavy sarcasm, and waved a hand at the tip that was my bedroom. "We're well on top of it. As you can see. Just another month or two, and we should have found homes for everything."

"Right." He took a tentative step forwards, and peered over the top of his glasses. "Only – forgive me for interfering – but d'you think it might be easier if you arranged the furniture first?"

I stared at him. "Arranged the furniture?"

"Yes. I could help bring in Molly's bed and wardrobe and so on, and you could both decide where they're going. Then everything else can be sort of slotted in. If you'd like me to help, that is."

Now why couldn't I have thought of that? Of course the furniture should have been brought in first; nothing else made sense. But I'd sooner have died than admitted that to Geoffrey.

There he stood in my doorway, tall and stooping and lanky, so well-meaning and full of good intentions. But whereas before he'd just been a visitor – a guest, one of the Nigels – he was now a permanent fixture. He was here for ever, and I resented his presence and his suggestions more than I could possibly put into words.

"Thanks," I said, as rudely as I dared, "but no thanks." And I stepped forwards and pushed the door shut, gently, in his face.

Rupert arrived some time during the afternoon. He came through the front door quite suddenly, carrying in his arms a large rectangular object covered with a cloth. Behind him was his father, laden with boxes apparently containing a computer, and puffing a little with the effort.

"Mattie darling, do go and help Geoffrey with those things," Mum said from behind me, but Geoffrey shook his head.

"No, no," he said, breathlessly. "I'm fine. I'm not sure Rupert trusts anyone other than me with his computer, anyway!"

He went on upstairs with his load, with Mum leading the way. Rupert and I exchanged looks. His was deadpan, with not a trace of expression. I don't know what mine was like.

"Quite right," I said pleasantly. "I'd probably drop it on the floor and smash it to bits."

Rupert moved his mouth slightly: you could hardly call it a smile.

"You might," he said.

"Yeah," I said. "And then I might jump on it and smash it some more."

The smile, or whatever it was, disappeared, and Rupert moved as if to go past me and up the stairs. I stepped aside with exaggerated politeness.

"After you," I said. "First on the right – but then, you know that, don't you? I think Molly's taken her nameplate off the door, but if she hasn't, just stick it in the bag of rubbish on the landing. She's not going to need it any more, is she?"

Rupert flushed, but didn't say anything. I stuck out a hand and touched the cloth that covered the thing he was carrying.

"What's this, then; your budgie?"

He smiled properly then, a nasty crafty little smile, and his eyes gleamed.

"No," he said, "my wat." And he whipped the cloth off in the manner of a conjuror performing a trick.

It was a rat, too. I caught sight of a sleek brown body and a revolting worm-like tail before Rupert threw the cloth back over the cage.

"Oh my God!" I clapped a horrified hand over my mouth as Mum came thundering down the stairs with Geoffrey and Molly in hot pursuit. I hadn't realized I'd screamed that loudly.

"Mattie, what on earth's the matter, darling? Are you all right?"

"He's got a rat," I managed to say, from behind my hand. I felt sick.

"I only showed her Colin," Rupert said, innocently. "She asked to see him, so I showed her."

Molly craned forward with interest. "Let's have a look."

Rupert lifted a corner of the cloth, and she peered inside, apparently fascinated. I could have kicked her.

"But it's a *rat*!" I took my hand away from my mouth. "He was taking it upstairs! He can't have a rat in his room, Mum: it's disgusting!"

"It's quite domesticated," Mum told me, with a placating little pat on the shoulder. I could have kicked her, too.

"What, you mean it makes the beds and does the washing-up?" I said, scathingly. "Mum, you don't understand – it's a *rat*. You know, bubonic plague, and all that!"

"Colin's a pet," Geoffrey put in, his voice loaded with reasonableness and calm good sense. "He's very clean, and tame. He won't hurt you, rest assured."

I was assured of no such thing. What sane person calls a rat Colin? Come to think of it, what sane person wants a rat for a pet anyway? I gave another shudder.

"Well, I think it's gross."

"Yes, darling, you've made that quite plain." Mum turned to Rupert with one of her best bright smiles, the kind she gives what she calls her less able students. "Why don't you take him upstairs now, Rupert? Get him settled in before supper time."

"If he escapes..." I began, warningly.

"He won't escape." Rupert shoved the thing under my nose, sadistically. "He's in a metal cage, look. And I always give him plenty to chew. It's only when they're bored they twy and gnaw their way out. Don't you know anything about wats?"

"No," I said, with as much dignity as I could muster. "I've got a life."

By supper time, Molly and I had got the room more or less tidy. At least, between us, we'd manhandled the furniture in, put Moll's clothes away and cleared the beds, and large patches of carpet were now visible between the larger mounds of detritus on the floor.

We'd just finished eating – all of us, squeezed around the oval pine kitchen table – when the telephone rang.

"I'll get it." I jumped up from the table immediately. "It'll be Jaz, wondering why I haven't been over."

Molly pouted. "But it's your turn to wash up. You'll be gassing away for ages, and I'll be lumbered with it."

"I'll do it." Rupert got to his feet and began stacking the dirty plates in a haphazard way. "I don't mind washing-up, Mrs Fwy. I quite enjoy it."

"Don't suck up to my mother!" I thought the words, but with enormous will power stopped myself saying them. It would only have caused a scene, and what use would that be?

Instead, I squeezed out a grudging "thanks", and went out to the hallway to answer the phone.

"*Bonjour, chérie!*" It was, as predicted, Jaz. "How's it going then?"

"Need you ask? I've spent all day clearing up my room to make space for Molly to turn it into a tip. It's totally pants."

"You sound in need of cheering up. Why don't you come over this evening? We could get a video."

Jaz's father is rolling in it, so consequently Jaz's room is stuffed with TVs, videos, computers, CD players – all the latest state-of-the-art technology, you name it, she's got it. As the technology in our house consists of one elderly television, a portable CD player and what Mum proudly calls a Music Centre (circa

1980, and complete with turntable), I don't usually need any encouragement to go round to Jaz's and check out her latest toy. However, something told me that today was different.

"I could," I began, slowly, "but I think Mum wants me to stay in tonight."

"Why?" I could hear the disappointment in her voice. "You always come over when you get back from holiday. I want to know how you got on with Tin Grin – and boy, have I got some hot goss for you!"

It was tempting, but I knew if I suggested it to Mum I'd have got her famous must-you-really look. She never actually forbids me to do things, she just looks sad and droopy and makes me feel like a selfish cow: it gets to me every time.

"Can't you tell me over the phone?"

"No way!" Jaz giggled. "You never know who might be listening."

"Oh, go on," I pleaded.

"Sorry. It'll have to wait." I could hear the faint sound of someone calling in the background. "Look, gotta go, my mobile's ringing. Give us a call when you're free, OK?" and she rang off.

I stood there with the buzzing receiver in my hand, wondering why my life was so dull. My so-called life. Why couldn't I have a mobile phone and high-tech toys in my room? Why couldn't I have lads queuing round the block to take me out, and be the first recipient (and possibly the perpetrator) of all the latest scandal?

Because it's not just my life that's dull, a little voice inside my head told me, *but I'm dull too*. What have I got? A house that's kilometres from anywhere and anyone, a shared room with my terminally untidy kid sister, a ditzy mother, and a stepfather and brother who look like escapees from Planet Boff.

Stunned by the unfairness of life, I replaced the receiver, only to have it ring again immediately. I snatched it up.

"Look, I'm sorry, but I really can't come out tonight, OK?" I snapped. Jaz had obviously finished with the caller on her mobile and had decided to have another go at persuading me to go over, and sod what my family expected. It occurred to me, in some dim recessed part of my brain, that my friend could sometimes be really selfish. It wasn't the first time she'd refused to take no for an answer.

"Can't you take no for an answer?" I added.

There was a stunned silence. "Is that Mattie?" a voice said at last. A *male* voice???

"Ye-es," I said, cautiously.

"So you can't come out, then?"

"Who *is* this?" I asked, suspiciously.

"It's me."

Wow. Helpful, or what? I hate it when people introduce themselves on the phone as "me", it's so egocentric. As if they think you only know one person: them.

"Oh, right. And which me would that be, then?" I treated him, whoever he was, to the full force of the Matilda Fry Irony Programme.

"Me. Sam."

Sam! I was so shocked I nearly dropped the phone.

"Sam! Oh my God, sorry – I thought, er, I was expecting someone else."

"Someone you didn't want to go out with?"

"Er, yes. Yes, that's right."

Well, what harm could it do? He might think I was being pestered by lads desperate to date me.

"So you didn't realize it was me?"

"No, I – um – I didn't recognize your voice. Listen, how did you get my number?"

"Jaz gave it to me."

And to think I'd been calling her selfish only minutes before! My wonderful, brilliant, helpful friend…

"So how about it then?" Sam's voice cut across my mental eulogizing.

"Sorry?"

He tutted impatiently. "Coming out with me."

"Oh, right. Yes, great, that would be fab, I'd like that, yes…" I bit my tongue, actually bit down on it, to stop myself gabbling any more.

"Cool. I'll come now then, yeah? I'll be about twenty minutes. Put something nice on, I hate girls in trousers."

I started to say that, when I'd said I'd like to go out with him, I hadn't actually necessarily meant in twenty minutes' time, but it was too late – he'd hung up. I toyed with the idea of dialling 1471 to get his number and ringing him back, explaining about the Hortons and it being the first night back and Mum's expectations, but it was no good; I couldn't face knocking Sam back a second time. I thought I'd blown it that time when he and Andy cycled all the way over to the cove. It was nothing short of miraculous that he'd asked me out a second time: I couldn't risk his patience or interest lasting for a third attempt.

Stuff Mum's expectations, I thought determinedly, and ran upstairs to rifle through my clothes for something suitable to wear. *I've fancied Sam Barker for ten months: Mum'll just have to manage without me this evening.*

chapter nine

God! I think I'm in love!! Sam is so cool and gorgeous. I can't believe I've just spent two hours with him, by myself!!! Much to my surprise, Mum didn't object to me going out this evening, although I had the third-degree when I got back. Sam and me walked up the hill to the Smugglers' Rest for a coffee, then back down to the cove and had a lovely romantic walk on the beach. First he held my hand, then he put his arm round me, then he started kissing me — honestly, we could hardly stop! He's such a top kisser. As we stood there the sun started to go down; it was just like something out of a film, I half expected violins to start playing (well, they were playing in my mind!!) He's asked me to the cinema on Sat. — can't wait!!!!!

It was unbelievably difficult to write the above entry, for two reasons: 1) Molly was hanging around my desk, attempting to look nonchalant but clearly trying to sneak a look over my shoulder and 2) I didn't want to write what had really happened. Not all of it, anyway. So I peppered my prose with as many exclamation marks as possible, to give Molly the general idea of a sensational and mind-blowing evening, and kept the real events to myself to mull over.

The truth was, I didn't know what to make of my date with Sam, or even if you could properly call it a date. I seemed to have been hankering after him for so long, swooning over his good looks and certain that I would never stand a chance of him asking me out, that I couldn't quite grasp the fact that the impossible had happened and he'd done just that. As if my brain hadn't had time to catch up with the reality of being in his company. And then there was just that – his company. I wasn't sure what to make of that, either. Things hadn't quite gone as I'd imagined they would.

"Hiya," I said, breezing out of the cottage. Mindful of his comment about girls in trousers, I'd dug out an old Lycra skirt I used to wear on the beach. It was a bit short, but it would have to do; no way was I borrowing any of Mum's karma skirts for a date with Sam Barker.

None of my T-shirts looked right with the skirt – too long and/or baggy – so I bribed Molly to lend me a black crop top I'd had my eye on for ages. My stomach was just about flat enough to get away with it.

"God," Molly said when she saw me, and

sucked her teeth. "What are you planning to do, sunbathe?"

"It's only the sort of thing *you* wear," I pointed out.

"Yeah, but you're bigger than me."

"Oh, thanks a bunch! You mean fatter." I turned round to get a glimpse of my back view. Perhaps she was right. Perhaps it was a bit much on me.

"No, I mean bigger. You know – *bigger*." She made curvy shapes in the air with her hands, and then giggled suddenly. "You look exactly like the sort of girl Sam Barker goes out with."

And it seemed she was right, because when Sam saw me a dirty great smile spread across his face.

"Hi," he said, in response.

"Well," I said.

"Well," he said back, and the grin spread even further.

"What shall we do, then?"

"I know what I'd *like* to do..."

"What's that?"

But he didn't answer, just grinned some more and then bent and fiddled with the back wheel of his bike. It looked like it was up to me to suggest our evening's programme, then. Perhaps that was the done thing when the date was on your home turf; my experience of dates being somewhat limited, I didn't really know what he expected.

"Shall we go up to the caff, then, and have a coffee?" I suggested.

"Can't we go indoors and have a coffee?"

I thought of what was indoors — Molly and her indiscreet comments, the chaos that was my room, Geoffrey, *Rupert* — and pulled a face. "Not really."

"Why not?"

I thought fast. "It's my stepfather; he's a bit…" I screwed up my nose, "…you know."

"Right. Gotcha. Where's this caff, then?"

I turned and pointed. "Up the lane — at the top, near the car park. You must have gone past it when you came down."

"At the top of that hill?" He looked disgruntled. "You mean I've got to go all the way up again? It must be one in four, easily. How are we supposed to get up there?"

I go up that hill practically every day of my life to catch the school bus, and stopped noticing the gradient years ago. I laughed: OK, perhaps just a tad sarcastically.

"Fly, of course! I thought you were supposed to be sporty; doesn't that keep you fit?"

"I *am* fit! I bet I'm fitter than you!" He looked annoyed, and the faintest bat squeak of warning sounded in my brain.

"I expect you are. Shall we find out? I'll race you to the top!"

He beat me by loads – I had to keep stopping to pull my skirt down over my bum – but at least it got us to the caff in record time. Unfortunately, I'd quite forgotten that it closes at seven in September, ready for total winter shut-down at the end of October, and it was now September the first. We just had time to gulp down a quick cappuccino (or what passes for it at the Smug's) before they chucked us out. Sam had a portion of chips as well.

"Missed my tea," he explained, shovelling the chips in as if he'd missed lunch, breakfast and tea the previous night as well.

"Back to school on Tuesday," I said, spooning the froth off my coffee and eating it.

Sam grimaced. "D'you have to? I wanted to enjoy this evening."

"Oh, sorry." I put the spoon down, contritely. "I just love the cocoa powder, you see."

"What?" He stared at me. "Oh, no – I meant, must you talk about school?"

"Sorry. What shall we talk about, then?"

He looked at me then, straight into my eyes, and a weird tingle of surprise passed through me. As his eyes met mine I noticed their colour; not the deep smouldering brown I'd

116

always thought them to be, but a light clear blue. Not that there's anything wrong with blue eyes, I'd just always thought they were brown. I felt curiously let down; ridiculous, as it was hardly Sam's fault I'd mistaken his eye colour.

"Mattie!"

"Sorry – what?" I was so busy staring at him I hadn't heard what he'd said.

"I said, why do we have to talk about anything? I've never been a great one for talking, me. Why don't we just go back down to the beach and – you know – get to know each other?"

I couldn't quite see how we could get to know each other without talking, but I soon found out. As soon as we were back down at the cove he was all over me like a rash.

"So that's what you meant by getting to know me," I giggled, trying to monitor his wandering hands.

"Yer wha'?" he muttered, thickly, his face buried in my neck.

"Getting to know each other," I said, and wriggled out of his grasp.

"Oh, yeah – it was a euphonium."

"A what?" I laughed. "Oh, right – you mean a euphemism."

His eyes narrowed (Warning No. 2), and he

117

moved away from me and sat down on a rock. He took a battered packet of Rothmans from the top pocket of his denim jacket, shook a cigarette from it and lit it in a practised fashion with a match in his cupped hand. After a moment or two he offered me the packet.

"Want one?"

I shook my head. "I don't, thanks."

"D'you do anything you shouldn't?" He took a long drag from the cigarette, held it, and then exhaled through his nostrils, half-closing his eyes against the smoke.

I was puzzled. "Sorry?"

"You don't smoke, you obviously didn't like –" He nodded his head towards the spot on the shingle where he'd been ravishing me thirty seconds earlier.

"Oh, I did," I said hurriedly. "I do." God forbid that I should spurn the advances of St Mark's legendary Lothario – the shame of it! It would be all over school that I was frigid.

He brightened. "You do?"

"Yes," I said, firmly. "I do. Definitely."

"Wicked," he said, and got off the rock. He ground out the cigarette with his heel. "In that case, why don't we go in that cave over there…?"

There followed, gentle reader, an interlude that I have no intention of describing, other than to say I enjoyed it very much, thank you (well, most of it, anyway: his hands continued to do rather more exploring than I was comfortable with). There was no doubt he was a pretty expert kisser, though: I'd certainly never been snogged so thoroughly before.

After an indeterminate period of time — ten minutes? an hour? a week? — we both came up for air.

"You know what?" Sam looked at me, and smiled. In the dim light of the cave his eyes could easily pass for the smouldering brown of my imagination. "You're something special."

I was delighted. "Am I?"

"Sure you are." He reached for me again, but I took a tiny half-step backwards.

"I'm just a bit confused about something."

"What's that, sugar?" His voice was low and husky, his face dreamy with pleasure.

"Well, as you're so into sport and everything, and obviously so good at it, and really fit..." He nodded, satisfied with this description of himself, and I pressed on. "How come you smoke?"

The expression on his face changed instantly and completely, like a blackboard being wiped.

"Because I like it," he said, shortly, and began to stride out of the cave. "My decision, OK?"

"Yes, sure," I said, scrambling along behind

him, my heart in my boots. What had I done? "I just thought—"

"Well, don't think," he snapped. "Thinking and girls don't go together. Not *my* girls, anyway."

So I was his girl, then? I wanted to ask him, but something stopped me, some tiny vestige of an unfamiliar, unrecognizable emotion.

We reached the lane, where he'd left his bike propped up against the garden wall, and he turned to me, his expression softer.

"We could go and see a movie on Saturday," he said, casually. "If you want."

Relief flooded me. "Oh, yes – yes please."

"OK then. I'll give you a ring." He stretched out a finger and touched my lips, gently, in a gesture that was both tenderly romantic and in total contrast to the passionate, almost frantic snogging in the cave. "See ya."

And he jumped on his bike and was gone, pedalling athletically up the hill.

Sam Barker's taking me to the cinema! He kissed me! He said I'm special! I hugged the thoughts to myself, deliciously, as I watched his rear view disappearing. Jaz was right. He did have a cute butt.

"Who was that?" Mum asked, as I floated into the kitchen thirty centimetres off the ground.

"Only Sam Barker," I said, perching on the edge of the table and trying to sound offhand.

Molly puffed out her cheeks. "Only the most fancied boy in the whole of St Mark's. Only a minor sex god. Only——"

"Yes, OK, thanks Molly. I'm sure Mum gets the picture," I cut across her. I wasn't sure I wanted Mum to know I'd just spent the last couple of hours with a sex god, minor or otherwise.

"Don't minor sex gods drink coffee, then?" Mum asked.

"Oh, that's OK; we had one up at the Smug's."

Mum leant towards me, and sniffed suspiciously. "You haven't been smoking, have you?"

"No!" I was truly appalled.

"It really messes you up, you know? Blocks your chi."

"De-synchronizes your yin and yang," I muttered. "I wouldn't, Mum – I hate the smell, you know I do."

"Yes, I do." Mum reached forward and ruffled my hair. "Is he nice, this Sam Barker?"

I smiled – I couldn't help myself, a great big grin just sort of spread itself across my chops. "Yes."

"Why don't you ask him in next time? There's no need for him to lurk around outside."

"He wasn't lurking!" I said, indignantly.

"Darling, don't be defensive. I wasn't meaning to imply anything, it's just that I like to meet your friends."

"So you can vet them," I muttered.

Mum went into put-out mode then, and started protesting that she never vets my friends and never would, it's up to me to decide who I want to be friendly with, she's always given me my space, etc. etc., until I got totally fed up of the topic.

"Look," I said, standing up, "I don't even know if there's going to be a next time; but if there is, I'll make sure you get to give him the seal of approval, OK?"

Molly followed me up the stairs. "You didn't have to say that to Mum," she said, offhandedly. "She's cool about who we hang out with, you know she is."

I gave a shrug. "If you say so."

"So what happened, then? Aren't you seeing him again?"

The grin slid over my face again; it was as if my mouth had a life of its own. "We're going to the cinema on Saturday."

"No kidding." She was clearly impressed. "Wow! So you're Sam Barker's latest, then. What happened this evening: what did you do?"

"They were snogging."

Molly and I both spun around. Rupert was standing in the doorway of his room – so recently Molly's room, it seemed odd and incongruous to see him there, framed in the doorway with his belongings as a backdrop.

"What?" I demanded. "How do you know? Did you follow us?"

Rupert pushed his glasses up on to the bridge of his nose with a forefinger. "I just went for a walk," he said, his face quite emotionless. "I wanted to go and explore the cave. I saw you both in there."

"You were spying on us!" I burst out. I felt quite hot at the thought of Rupert watching Sam and me locked together at the lips – and everything else…

Rupert and I looked at each other for a long moment. Then, without his expression changing one iota, he turned and went back into the room, closing the door quietly behind him.

Molly was agog. "Did you?" she demanded, avidly. "Did you snog Sam Barker? What was it like? Was he—?"

"Oh for God's sake," I said icily, from the height of my three years' seniority over my sister, "grow up, will you? Of course he kissed me. It's what people our age do when they go out together."

And I went into our room and sat down at

my desk, pointedly, and began to write in my diary.

The thing was, despite just having lived out one of my major fantasies, despite having got to snog Sam Barker and thoroughly enjoying the experience: despite all that, I didn't feel as euphoric and cloud-niney as I'd been anticipating. Little things kept coming back to me, little scenes replaying in my mind: Sam's passionate brown eyes turning out to be blue, his peevishness at having to go back up the hill to the caff. Him shovelling those chips into his mouth. The faint taste of vinegar and cigarettes as he kissed me. His anger when I asked him why he smoked. His comment about girls and thinking not going together. It all left me feeling faintly uneasy. Almost — it was ridiculous, I knew, not to mention unfair, but I almost felt disappointed, as if Sam had let me down by being the person he was, rather than the person I'd thought he was.

But I didn't want to feel disappointed, I wanted to savour the experience. Pushing the thoughts to the back of my brain, I got down to writing my diary entry. *After all*, I told myself smugly, *it's not everyone who gets to date a minor sex god*.

chapter ten

I had very mixed feelings about school starting again. On the one hand, Rupert was going to be there. Geeky, friendless, ex-prep school Rupert; it couldn't be long before news got out that he was my new stepbrother, and how would that reflect on me? I was, quite frankly, dreading it.

But on the other hand, acting as a counterbalance, was Sam. (*My boyfriend*, as I kept dreamily reminding myself. *Mine*.) The cinema had been a resounding success. We'd gone to see the latest James Bond, but it could have been the latest Mickey Mouse for all the notice we'd both taken of the film. Entwined satisfactorily together on the back row (that old cliché), and then again in the bus all the way back, I was pleasantly surprised to discover how little we needed to talk to, well, get to know each other, as Sam had put it. And now, remembering the assorted glamorous females he usually had draped around him at school, I was looking forward to being the latest. What a boost to my reputation *that* would be! Perhaps it would make up, just a bit, for the Rupert Factor.

Guess what? It didn't happen like that. For a start, the first day back I hardly saw Rupert all day (which was good). For a second, I hardly saw Sam either. Which wasn't.

When I'd had my romantic visions of us swanning mistily around school together, hand in hand, I'd forgotten one small thing. Sam was now in the sixth form, which at our school means all free lessons and spare time is spent in the Sixth Form Block. The Sixth Form Block requires capital letters, even when you're saying it rather than writing it: it takes itself majorly seriously. To enter the Sixth Form Block when you're only in year eleven is a hanging offence, as Jaz pointed out after lunch when I was getting mega browned-off with only spotting my beloved from afar.

"There's only one thing to do to get to see him," I declared, marching her up the stairs.

"You can't go in there!" she said, aghast.

"Why not?" I demanded, my hand on the sacred portal.

"You're not allowed – you'll break their *cordon sanitaire!*"

"I'm not contaminated."

"You are to them. They think anyone not in

their little clique is polluted. Anyway, has it occurred to you he might be trying to avoid you?"

That did it. "Stuff that," I said, and pushed the door open before I lost my nerve.

The Sixth Form Block is situated above the Upper School dining room and is surrounded with windows, which means everyone inside can see you as you climb the stairs to it. I guess it's the modern equivalent of arrow slits and ramparts; sure enough, someone was posted at the door to repel all boarders as I pushed it open.

"What do you want?" she enquired, frostily. (It would be a she.)

"I'm looking for Sam Barker," I said, as confidently as I could manage.

She gave an irritatingly knowing smile. "Not another one! Sam," she called, over her shoulder. "One of your little admirers to see you."

Craning my neck to see past her, I could just make out the figure of Sam as he detached himself from a small group, most of them girls. He came loping over in that familiar sexy way, and my stomach turned over.

"Hi," I said, fondly.

He glanced at Jaz and me, in that order. "Oh, hello." (Was it my imagination, or didn't he exactly sound pleased to see me?)

"I just thought I'd come and find you."

He nodded. "Right."

"Only I haven't seen you at all today – not to talk to, I mean."

"Well, it's the first day back, isn't it?"

I couldn't see what difference that made. "What d'you mean?"

A tiny frown crossed his brow. "I mean there's A level classes to sort out. Settling down in here." He made a slightly impatient sweeping gesture towards the Sixth Form Block. "Things like that."

"I see."

I must have sounded as dejected as I felt, because his face softened. "Look, I'll try and see you after school, OK? Just for a moment or two. Can't promise anything, though."

Suddenly, the sun came out. "OK."

"See you then, gorgeous." He touched my cheek, briefly, and then turned and went back into the sacred Inner Sanctum.

"Boy oh boy." Jaz shook her head, sadly. "You have got it bad."

But Jaz's teasing couldn't touch me: the girl sentry had heard Sam call me Gorgeous and was now looking with grudging respect in my direction. It kept me going all afternoon.

After school, however, there was no sign of him, despite my hanging round pointedly outside the SFB until I could hang around no longer because Molly came to dig me out.

"There you are," she grumbled. "I've been looking everywhere for you. The bus is just about to leave, you're going to miss it if you don't come now."

The choice was simple: stay on the off chance of seeing Sam and walk the six kilometres home, or go on the bus. The bus won – yeah, I know I've said I like walking, but I don't like it *that* much. Not carrying my school bag, which weighs about three tonnes. Not when it's raining, which it had just started to do, and I didn't have a coat. And not when I had no guarantee that I'd even get to see Sam if I stayed.

I was just getting to the front of the rugby scrum that passes for the school bus queue when I felt a tap on my shoulder, and someone called my name. I turned. It was Sam.

He pulled me from the mass of bodies and, putting his arms around my waist, began to kiss me. The pit of my stomach gave a lurch, and I kissed him back with enthusiasm.

"When you two have finished slurping each other," the bus driver said sardonically, after a longish interval, "I'd quite like to get away. If that's all right with you both."

"Put her down, Sam," someone yelled from the interior of the bus, and everyone laughed.

I pulled away from him, reluctantly. "Better go," I whispered.

He smiled. "See you soon, yeah?"

"Can you come over this evening?"

"Difficult." He shook his head. "I don't think so. I'll see you at school tomorrow."

I got on the bus and sat in my usual place, next to Jaz, wishing as I did so that Sam didn't live so close to school and had to use the bus too. Sitting next to him mornings and evenings would improve our relationship no end, I thought wistfully.

I watched him stride along the pavement outside school, his bag hitched over one shoulder, as the bus gathered momentum along the road. In the split second of passing him I thought I saw a person detach itself from the hedging around the school entrance and join Sam as he walked by. I had a brief image of swinging blonde hair and a flash of short skirt and long legs (a *female* person…), but I could have been mistaken. I told myself it was just coincidence, just another pupil leaving at the same time as him.

"Happy now?" Jaz enquired, her eyebrows raised, as the bus drove round a corner and left Sam behind.

"Ecstatic, thanks for asking."

My lips still tingled from his kiss. He wasn't

avoiding me. He'd come to find me, in the bus queue, and kissed me in front of everyone. It wasn't much, but it was enough.

It seemed to set the tone for our relationship. I soon realized that my romantic dream of us hanging out together at school was just that — a dream. Sam was far too busy with being in the sixth form to pay me much attention at school; I told myself I should have foreseen it, as the sixth formers at St Mark's are famously elusive. They're far too busy doing sixth-formy things in their groovy Sixth Form Block to be spotted around the corridors much.

We still saw each other after school, though, and at weekends. (Occasionally after school, and the odd weekend, to be strictly accurate.) These meetings would usually follow the same pattern: Sam would ring me up, mostly out of the blue, and then cycle round immediately for a mammoth snogging session.

Put like that, candidly, in black and white, it looks terrible, doesn't it? But the truth was, I was quite happy with the situation. As time went by and the days grew shorter and the weather colder, we abandoned the cave on the beach in favour of my bedroom; my/Molly's bedroom, of course, but Moll would usually decamp slightly huffily downstairs to do her homework or watch the telly, and leave us in peace. So we were warm, and comfortable, and relatively undisturbed: and pretty early on I realized that Sam had been right when he'd said, that first evening in the caff, that he wasn't a great one for talking. We scarcely talked at all. Mind you, there's a limit to how much chatting you can do when you're joined at the lips for much of the evening.

As I say, though, I was happy enough: at least at the beginning. It was enough for me that people at school seemed to know Sam and I were an item. On the few occasions when he acknowledged me publicly – put an arm round me, sought me out after a class or in the bus queue – I felt myself swell with pride, with the kudos of being one of Sam Barker's Chosen Few. And I never got tired of kissing him – never would, I told myself fervently. It never occurred to me, then, that I shouldn't have been happy with the relationship: that it couldn't even properly be called a relationship, that the Chosen Few were more of a multitude than a few, and that the reason for their being chosen was, for the most part, decidedly dodgy.

It occurred to Jaz, though. Annoyingly, she kept pointing it out to me.

"You shouldn't let him ignore you like that,"

she would tell me, as he passed by in the distance yet again. Or, "How can you let him treat you like that?" as he plucked me from the bus queue for another long, lingering kiss goodbye.

"Like what?"

"Like you're just there for his convenience. Like you've got no feelings, and he can just pick you up and put you down when he chooses. He's just using you, Mattie – can't you see that?"

"He isn't," I protested.

"No? How come I only see you together at school when he chooses, then? What d'you do when you go out with him? Where does he take you?"

"God, Jaz, what is this – the Spanish Inquisition? I'm happy, OK?"

"Well, you shouldn't be," she persisted. "It's degrading. It demeans you, being treated like Sam Barker's love toy."

I grinned at that, but she was deadly serious. What she couldn't seem to grasp was the fact that I felt neither demeaned nor degraded by Sam's treatment of me. That perhaps I was using him, too. That, whatever Jaz thought of Sam, I had a choice as well, and I was choosing to spend time with him.

The fact was, he was one of the few people I

could choose to have around me these days. At home, crammed together in the little cottage that had been plenty big enough when it was just Mum and Molly and me living there, we all seemed to be falling over each other. Everyone was getting on my nerves. Molly and I had always got on tolerably well, but sharing a bedroom just wasn't working out. She was so untidy, and I was used to having things just the way I wanted them. Geoffrey was drifting around being infuriatingly non-partisan about anything and everything, from what colour Rupert should paint his bedroom walls to what we should have for supper, so incredibly keen was he not to upset anyone or rock the boat. Rupert: well, Rupert continued to be Rupert. Just looking at him was enough to set my teeth on edge, with his neat, miniature-adult appearance and his supercilious expression. Luckily, I didn't see him around school much, and was able to ignore him on the bus as he always sat with Michael Stewart. I supposed he'd settled in at St Mark's: it was hard to tell, really, as he never said anything when we got home, just shut himself in his room for hours on end to play on his precious computer.

Even Mum was starting to give me a hard time, mostly about Sam. Perhaps she and Jaz had been swapping notes. The basis of her complaints seemed to be his lack of conversation. It all came to a head one evening just after half-term, when Sam had gone home after the usual couple of hours in my room largely spent exploring my tonsils.

"I can't help noticing how often you two just disappear upstairs when Sam comes round," she said.

I shrugged. "So?"

"So it would be good to talk to him occasionally."

"Mum," I said, patiently. "He's seventeen. You're forty. What would you talk about?"

"I'm thirty-nine. And I'm not asking for in-depth conversation, just a word or two occasionally."

"He doesn't really do small talk." I opened the fridge and took out a yoghurt. "Has Molly nicked all the strawberry ones again? Typical."

"He must talk to you," Mum persisted. "What kind of things do you two discuss?"

I shrugged again, and peeled the foil lid off the yoghurt. "This and that. Nothing you'd be interested in."

"Well, what subjects is he doing at school? What about his family? Has he got any hobbies?"

Snogging me, I thought, licking the lid. *What would she say if I told her that*? I suppressed a grin. "Search me. We've never discussed his hobbies. Oh yeah – sport. He's good at sport." I looked closely at Mum. "Look, what is this? You're not seriously telling me you want to chat with him about the chances of him captaining the Under Eighteens next season?"

"No, of course not." She sounded exasperated, though I couldn't imagine why. I'd already told her that Sam wasn't the world's greatest conversationalist. What could I do about it?

"I think what Alice means," Geoffrey put in, mildly, "is that hello and goodbye every now and then would be appreciated."

I spun round. I hadn't seen him standing in the doorway. "Really?" I said, frostily.

"That's all," he said, and smiled in a friendly way at me. "It's not a lot to ask, really, is it?"

I was filled with fury. Geoffrey had never, ever intervened before; the fact he was doing so now, however gently, ignited a sudden and inexplicable rage within me.

"Will you get off my case?" I shouted. "What's it got to do with you, anyway?"

Mum took a step forward, placatingly. "Mattie…"

"What?" I whirled round to face her. "It's none of his business! He's not my father!"

I slammed the yoghurt pot down on the kitchen table, violently; it fell on its side, and began haemorrhaging sticky white goo on to the floor.

"Of course not…" Geoffrey began, kindly, and put a hand out to me, but I pushed past him and ran upstairs.

Luckily, Molly wasn't in the bedroom: she was closeted in the bathroom, wallowing in the bath with a facepack and the radio on. I could hear her, singing along unself-consciously to Radio One. I threw myself down on the bed and lay there with clenched teeth, breathing heavily. What was it I was feeling? I wasn't upset, that was for sure. I was angry. *Angry angry angry…*

There was a tap on the door, a timid little knock. *Mum*, I thought. *Come to — what? Make amends? Reason with me? Hit me lightly about the face and body?* I hadn't a clue what to expect. Reluctantly, I got off the bed and opened the door.

It wasn't Mum. It was Rupert, his face expressionless as ever.

"What do you want?" I demanded.

He blinked, in his reptilian way. "I heard shouting."

"Oh dear. Pardon me for disturbing you."

"Are you all wight?"

I stared at him. "Like you care. Just shove off, will you!"

He stared right back at me. The muscles of his face didn't move, but I thought I saw something flare briefly behind his eyes. Then he turned wordlessly on his heel and went.

Good riddance, I thought to myself, pushing down the small puff of guilt that rose in me. *He was only being nosey, wanting to know what all the racket was about. He couldn't care less if I'm all right or not.*

I'd only been back in the room five seconds when there was another knock on the door. *If that's Wupert again…* I threw it open aggressively, ready to give him a right earful. This time, however, it was Mum. My angry comments died on my lips. "Oh," I said instead, lamely.

"Can I come in?"

"I suppose." I stepped back, holding the door open, and in she came. She stood there on the carpet between the two beds, Molly's and mine, looking faintly uneasy.

"I'm not going to apologize to Geoffrey," I said, stubbornly. "He shouldn't have stuck his oar in. It was nothing to do with him."

Mum made an impatient gesture, a small movement of her shoulders. "It's over, Mattie. Let it go. Don't – *prolong* things."

I scowled. "Then what have you come up here for?"

138

She sat down then, suddenly, on Molly's bed, and took something from the pocket of her voluminous patchwork skirt. She held it in her hand, uncertainly, for a moment; and then, with a rueful twist of her lips, held it out to me.

"This came this morning."

"What is it?" I bent my head to look at it.

"It's a letter. From your father. He wants to see you and Molly."

chapter eleven

Was I surprised? Was King Harold surprised
when that arrow got him in the eye at the
Battle of Hastings? I was astonished, flabber-
gasted, stunned — gobsmacked. A thousand
thoughts and memories jostled for position in
my brain, none of them good. All I could think
of to say was, "How did he find us?"

Mum made a brief dismissive gesture, as if
brushing something unpleasant off her skirt.
"He's always known how to find us."

"But…" I was aware of my mind working,
could literally feel my brain creaking and
clanking as if driven by cogs and ratchets. "But
I always thought you'd left him — that we'd run
away."

"Off into the deep dark night?" Mum gave a
tired little smile that didn't quite reach her
eyes. "You always did enjoy a spot of melo-
drama. I sent him this address shortly after we
moved here; I had to do the right thing, Mattie,
or it could have affected the divorce settle-
ment. And he was still your father, when all
was said and done." She sighed, and looked

down at the letter she still held. "He's always known how to find us. He just hasn't bothered, until now."

"So why's he bothering now, then?" I burst out. "What's the big deal?"

"You'd better read the letter," Mum said, and left me to it, but it didn't really tell me much. Certainly not why he'd decided – after, what? Five years? Six? – that he wanted to see his long-lost daughters again.

The letter was short, an envelope with unfamiliar exotic stamps containing a single sheet of airmail paper bearing an address in Kuwait. *Kuwait!* I thought. *Of course – oil!* I had a sudden flash of memory, of him talking, years ago, about oil rigs and the grimness of the winter weather in Aberdeen. That would explain his long absences from home.

The handwriting was small and cramped and not easy to read, and explained in a few terse sentences that his circumstances had changed, that he was coming back to visit England in the summer, and that he would like to see us: or as he put it, "my daughters Matilda and Molly", as if to distinguish us from his other daughters. Maybe he did have other daughters. Maybe he had a whole flotilla of other offspring secreted away somewhere, and other wives too. Who knew? Who cared?

141

Certainly not Molly, who refused point-blank to have anything to do with him. She wouldn't even look at the letter.

"But aren't you curious?" I asked her. "Aren't you just the teensiest bit intrigued about what he's like now, and why he wants to see us again, all of a sudden?"

"No," she said, simply.

"You must be. I don't believe you."

"You don't have to believe me. I don't want to see him. Full stop."

"Ah, come on Moll," I wheedled. "Surely you must be a little bit interested. I know I am."

"Well I'm not." She looked at me, sharply. "Just because you think something, it doesn't mean everybody else has to, you know."

I blinked. "Meaning?"

"Look Mat, if you want to see him, you go ahead. Just count me out, that's all. Besides—" She stopped, and chewed on her bottom lip.

"Besides what?"

"Well – d'you think it would be fair on Mum?"

"Fair?" I was temporarily speechless. "What, like now she's got Geoffrey we've got to accept him as our dad, too?"

"Of course not." She clicked her tongue. "Why do you have to be so – so *confronting*?"

"Confrontational," I said, automatically.

142

"Whatever. Geoffrey's OK, you know he is. He's never tried to be our dad; that's well unfair."

"Hark at Miss Justice of the Year!" I exclaimed. "So it's not you who's been inciting gangs of little kids to call Rupert names, then?"

"Ah," she said, and blushed.

I'd noticed them at school several times, small knots of year sevens trailing along behind Rupert in the playground and taunting him. I thought I'd recognized Molly's hand in the things they'd been shouting.

"I didn't exactly incite them," she explained. "One of them overheard me calling him Tin Grin and thought it was funny, that's all. You know what those kids are like."

Those kids were a whole year younger than her. "Oh, sure – not mature like you and me."

"Ha ha," she said, and pulled a face. "Anyway, you know Rupert – he doesn't take the slightest bit of notice. He asks for it, really. If only he'd respond, get upset or something, you'd feel sorry for him and tell them to stop picking on him."

I thought, briefly, of the time in the Lake District when he had responded. He'd got upset then, all right, and all we had both felt was contempt.

But as a rule, Molly has a much kinder heart

than me, as well as a more forgiving nature: which made it all the more difficult for me to understand her unilateral dismissal of our father's plea from Kuwait to be allowed to see us again.

As for me, I couldn't make up my mind what to do. I ended up putting the letter away, shoving it out of sight into my undies drawer, but I didn't forget about it; and as the weeks passed its folds became more marked, the paper ever flimsier, as I read and re-read it and tried to divine my father's motivation and intentions from the few functional words it contained.

Just before the end of the Christmas term, Rupert came up to me in the corridor at school as I was on my way to a lesson.

"Excuse me," he said, politely, as if it was the first time we'd met, rather than having shared a house with me for the last four months.

I turned round. Usual pasty face, usual slicked-down hair, usual heavy, unflattering glasses. A thrill of distaste passed through me.

"What do you want?"

"Yo, Tin Grin, how's it hangin'?" Bradley Smythe yelled out, pushing past us and going through the open classroom door without waiting for an answer.

Rupert didn't react, just stood there impassively. He never reacted to being taunted or called names, even though it sometimes seemed as if the whole school had cottoned on to the Tin Grin thing. It was almost a surprise if ever I overheard anyone calling him by his proper name.

"Have you got Maths next?" he asked me, and nodded towards the classroom Brad had disappeared into. "In there?"

I eyed him suspiciously. "What's it to you?"

He didn't answer my question. "With Mr Simkins?" he persisted.

"That's right. Maths, in there, with Mr Simkins. Now, is there anything else I can tell you about my timetable? Like, after lunch it's double English with Mrs Whittaker? Or maybe you're more interested in—"

But he walked briskly into the classroom, leaving me standing there. I could see Mr Simkins approaching along the corridor, so I had no choice but to follow Rupert into the room without being able to quiz him on what he thought he was doing in there.

I soon found out. As soon as the teacher got into the room, he turned to address the class.

"The more observant amongst you," he said, pompously, "might have noticed we have a new addition to the class. Rupert Horton," he waved a vague hand in Rupert's direction, "will be joining us for the rest of the academic year. Please don't be too unkind to him: the headmaster has already told him what a helpful, friendly bunch you are, and we don't want to disappoint him, do we?"

He didn't mean it literally: it's just the way old Simkins always talks, pillock that he is. But I got to my feet immediately.

"Please, Sir," I said. "I think there's been a mistake."

"Mistake? No, there's no mistake." He looked disgruntled, as if I'd challenged him about one of his famous calculations. But I pressed on.

"He's only thirteen," I said. "Won't this class be a bit — well — a bit advanced for him?"

Simkins looked at me over the top of his glasses. "Ah," he said. "I see. Young Matilda, looking out for your stepbrother, eh? Well, admirable though your sentiments are, I can assure you that Rupert won't find the work too advanced. He will be sitting his Maths GCSE in the summer term, along with the rest of you. Now, if that's all, perhaps you would sit down and allow us to get on with the lesson."

I sat down, mortified, blushing to the roots of my hair. Trust old Simkins, the pompous prat, and his big mouth; at least half the class had, up until then, no idea that Rupert was my stepbrother. My only very minor consolation was that, despite careful arrangement of his features into his usual bland expression, Rupert's face too was as red as a tomato. I didn't know if it was caused by the revelation (to some) about our stepsibling status or simply the unwarranted attention drawn to him; but it occurred to me, for the first time, that Rupert's non-reaction to things might simply be a façade, that he might have trained his face, over the years, not to betray his inner feelings.

Not that I cared, one way or the other. I was more concerned with the fact of actually having to put up with him in Maths: having him in one of *my* classes that, given that I was two years older than him, should have been a guaranteed Rupert-free zone.

Finding Mum unexpectedly in, sorting dirty laundry on the kitchen floor, when I got home after school that afternoon, I had a moan to her about it.

"It's like he's following me around, or something. Like he's been planted there to make sure I do all my Maths properly, like a good girl."

I threw my bag down on the floor with a grimace.

"But you do know that's not the reason he's there, don't you?"

"Of course I do! I'm not stupid. It's just how it feels, that's all."

"And why do you think that is?"

I considered it. "I don't know. I suppose – I suppose it feels like he's showing me up. Like, I'm really thick, but he's clever enough to do GCSE Maths at the age of thirteen."

Mum nodded sympathetically. "It must be tough to feel like that. But do you really think that's how everyone else sees it? His cleverness as a foil to your thickness?"

I didn't really care how everyone else saw it. I shrugged, irritably. "It's how I feel; can't you see that?"

"Yes, I can, but I'm sure nobody else—" She stopped suddenly, a small spasm of pain crossing her face, and put a hand up to her jaw. "Ow!"

"Are you OK?"

"Fine. It's just the anaesthetic wearing off."

"What anaesthetic?"

"I've just been to the dentist – root canal work. It's why I'm home early, darling – I'm sure I told you this morning."

I'd completely forgotten about it. Truth to tell, I'd been so tied up with my own moans I hadn't even thought to ask her why she was home early. It made me feel bad; before, I'd always have thought to ask Mum about her visits to the dentist, just as she would have

148

asked about mine. Before the Invasion from Planet Horton.

Mum looked round the kitchen suddenly, in a puzzled way. "So where's Molly and Rupert, then? Are they still at school?"

I bit back my usual, don't-you-ever-remember-anything-that-goes-on? type comment: I somehow didn't feel I had a leg to stand on.

"Moll's gone to Chloë's for tea, and Michael Stewart's asked Rupert to play with his new computer game. They told you this morning."

Mum threw a pillowcase into the washing machine with a little laugh. "Right pair, aren't we? Perhaps we ought to get a bulletin board for the kitchen, then everyone can write down what their plans are for each day."

"We'd probably forget to read it."

"Probably." Mum looked at me, her head to one side, and smiled suddenly with a smile that was full of love. "It's nice to have you here to myself for a little while, Mattie. I feel we've kind of lost each other a bit over the past few months."

I felt suddenly embarrassed. I knew what she meant, but I still felt embarrassed. I looked down at my feet, and said nothing.

"You do know I'm always here for you, don't you, darling? If ever you want to talk about anything?"

I gave a small, non-committal nod. The trouble was, the things I wanted to talk about, I doubted she wanted to hear. "Sure."

Mum smiled again, and then looked down at the dirty washing, heaped about her feet. "Love, could you do me a favour? I need Rupert's sheets to put in the machine; could you go and strip his bed for me, and make it up with the clean ones?"

I'd never been into Rupert's room; at least, not since it had stopped being Molly's. The first thing that struck me was how tidy it was — obsessively orderly, like the kind of fake bedroom you see in DIY stores, designed simply to show off the furniture. Everything had been put away, every surface completely clear of clutter; no clothes lying around, no school books or CDs or personal bits and pieces, nothing at all. The only signs that it was a real bedroom rather than a showcase one were a pair of slippers placed precisely together beside the bed, the computer screen winking away on the desk, and the rat's cage, surprisingly immaculately clean and odourless on a large sheet of newspaper underneath the window. *Colin*. I'd forgotten all about him. I approached the cage gingerly: I could just about make out his shape, asleep under a pile of wood shavings. That was all right, then: I wouldn't have to worry about fending off the Killer Rat.

I turned towards the bed, the duvet cover perfectly smooth and wrinkle-free as if its occupant ironed it each morning after sleeping under it, the clean linen sitting in a neat pile on the foot of the bed waiting to be put on it, when my eye was caught by Rupert's computer.

OK. I lie. I was snooping, I admit it. It was really quite innocent, though: I just thought I'd fiddle with the mouse for a bit, see what sort of thing he had stored, when I suddenly saw the name FRY as a desktop folder. Well, I had to see what *that* was all about, didn't I?

I clicked on to it. This is what came up on the screen.

RETURN OF THE MIGHTY TY'N GRHYN:
<u>in which the fearless Hero Warrier</u>
<u>defeats the Kingdom of Fry and its</u>
<u>Harridan Bitch-Queen M'Atil Da'aa.</u>
The mighty Ty'n Grhyn strode across
the dessolate alien landscape with
a careless sneer playing about his
lips. His manly jaw was set with a
granit resolve. He was mindful of
the oath he had sworn the previos
day, that by nightfall he would

151

have rid the world of the Bitch-Queen M'Atil Da'aa.

"Aye and her cohorts, to — by the Curse of Zando I will this very eventide" he mutered rougly to himself as he strode. His mind wandered painfuly back to battles past, battles fought with Al Iss, the Matriach Harridan (now a bit old and past it) and the young harridan-in-waiting Molifrei. How he had pitted his wits against there's, intelectualey they were no match for him and now he would prove his superier pysical strength to.

"Its three against one but I dont care, ha ha" he laughed carlessly. He well knew what was at steak. The hand of the beautifull and lovley maiden J'Asmil Aa (who was secretely in love with him but dared not admit it for fear of incuring the wroth of the Bitch-Queen), the Kingdom of Fry, yes even his life!

A big terible shuder passed through him. No not my life he thought bravley, for I am the mighty Ty'n Grhyn and there is no Harridan

alive that can defeat me! He felt
for his sword his sheild and his
laser zapper. All present and
correct. Now I am ready he thought,
and with that thought he

"Mattie, are you all right up there?" Mum's
voice came drifting up the stairs.

"Fine: I'm just doing Rupert's bed, I'll be
down in a tick."

I exited hurriedly, and the fearless Hero
Warrior disappeared from the screen to be
replaced by the swirling geometrical shapes of
the screen saver. So that's what he'd been doing
all those times he'd said he'd been working on
his computer! Concocting pathetic little
fantasy worlds for him to dominate. And pretty
lengthy ones too, judging by the amount of
memory the document was apparently taking
up — it must go on for pages and pages. What
kind of warped mind must he have?

As I stripped Rupert's bed I felt a hot surge
of fury: *how dare he call us harridans, just how dare
he! And as for calling me the Bitch-Queen...* I
ripped off the duvet cover and chucked it on
the floor. I had a good mind to confront him
about it, or better still to add something of my
own to his poxy little story, make his stupid
character M'Atil Da'aa win the battle, just to

let him know I was on to him.

But almost immediately I realized that wasn't the answer. I already had the answer in my hand, here in this room. Rupert didn't know I had read his creation, penetrated his secret world as it were, and that gave me power over him, even if I couldn't reveal I'd been snooping around among his private things. All the while he was unaware of my discovery, I could continue to find out what he really thought of us. *So he fancies Jaz, does he*, I thought grimly. *In your dreams, Mighty Ty'n Grhyn. M'Atil Da'aa has sussed you, my lad. And your spelling and punctuation suck, quite frankly.*

I yanked off the pillowcase and marched downstairs with my arms full of his dirty bed-linen. I was damned if I was going to make up his bed for him as well: he could bloody well do it himself.

chapter twelve

Extract from my diary, Boxing Day:

They say Christmas is for kids, and I guess that makes me a big kid because I've always loved it. Up until this year, that is. This year I finally got to grow up, and Christmas is never going to be the same.

We should have known, really, that it wasn't going to work. The atmosphere in our house wasn't exactly like The Waltons when we were all coming and going, living our usual day-to-day lives and hardly ever all there at once: how on earth could we expect to start playing Happy Families and pretend we were each other's best friends, just because it was Christmas and we were all thrown together for days on end?

Call me cynical, but I knew that was never going to happen. But Mum thought it would, I know, or perhaps she just hoped it, which I suppose isn't quite the same thing.

It started with the turkey. Or rather, the lack of it. I went into the kitchen one morning at the start of the holidays to find Mum and Geoffrey having a disagreement.

"But we've always had turkey at Christmas," Geoffrey was saying.

"We don't," Mum replied. "We never have."

"But it's traditional."

"Not in our house."

Eh up, I thought, taking the orange juice from the fridge and pouring some into a glass. *Could this be a row?*

"Morning," I said, cheerily. They both ignored me.

"Christmas isn't Christmas without turkey," Geoffrey continued.

"It is to us. We're vegetarian, Geoffrey. Factory-reared turkey has no place on our table."

"You don't have to eat it. You don't even have to cook it. I'm quite happy to do that. Besides, Rupert would be so disappointed to have nut roast for Christmas dinner."

Up until then it had all been quite reasonable and civilized.

"We never have nut roast," Mum objected, her voice rising by several decibels. "That's such a cliché. This is a matter of principle, not some 'you versus us' thing. Why must you emotionally blackmail me by bringing Rupert into it?" And then her face crumpled and she sat down, heavily, on to one of the spoonback pine kitchen chairs.

I stood by the fridge, orange juice carton in hand, riveted to the spot by an odd mixture of emotions, embarrassment and exhilaration and something that felt peculiarly like fear, although I couldn't think what there was to be frightened about.

Geoffrey sat down beside her and put an arm about her shoulders. "Love, I'm so sorry," he murmured. He seemed oblivious to my presence: they both did. "I didn't mean to – I didn't think – I was only…"

God, I thought in disgust, putting the orange juice away. *Can't he just finish a sentence? He would drive me insane.*

I picked up my glass and went out of the kitchen. Geoffrey was saying "of course we don't need a turkey", and Mum was saying "of course you must have a turkey, if you want one", and they were getting all touchy-feely with each other. *God!* It seemed like a mighty big fuss to make about a turkey. I remembered when Mum used to get that upset about world famine and animal experimentation and the hole in the ozone layer, and was never bothered much by the stupid little things my friends' parents were always getting their knickers into a twist about. It struck me that perhaps Geoffrey wasn't as good for Mum as she seemed to think he was.

Then there was another argument, about the Christmas tree. A couple of days after the turkey incident Geoffrey came staggering into the cottage, beaming, and bearing an enormous spruce.

Mum said, "Goodness," a little faintly, and put a hand to her throat. "It's very *large*, isn't it. Where will it go?"

"In the hallway," Rupert declared. "We always put our twee in the hallway, don't we, Dad."

"Oh, no!" Molly looked horrified. "It has to go in the sitting room, by the window."

Out of the corner of my eye I saw Mum and Geoffrey exchanging glances.

"How about the bathroom, for a change?" I suggested brightly. "Or – I know – why not the kitchen? To hell with what we've always done – let's be really different this year!"

Mum pressed her lips together, ever so slightly, and then turned to Geoffrey.

"We could try the hall, but I think it's too big."

It was. Unless we spent the entire Christmas downstairs, that is: it would have completely blocked the foot of the stairs. So it ended up in the sitting room, much to Molly's satisfaction.

"And the kids can decorate it," said Geoffrey.

I bridled slightly at being called a kid, but hey

— it was Christmas, after all. Goodwill to all men, etc. etc. Decorating the tree had always been one of the small pleasures of the time of year, and I wanted this year to be the same, even if we did have to let Rupert join in.

Molly appointed herself director of operations. She appeared in the sitting room with our old cardboard carton of decorations, rescued from the loft with all the attendant annual ceremony, at roughly the same time Rupert arrived cradling a box that was almost a twin to Molly's.

Molly looked at it. "What's that?"

"Our decowations."

"Oh, we won't need those," she declared, with a decisive toss of her head. "We've got plenty."

Rupert took no notice, but rummaged around in his box and began taking out plastic boxes of baubles and strings of tinsel.

"Oh God, we're not having tinsel!" Molly exclaimed. "Naff, or what!"

"Darlings, don't squabble," Mum said, with an anxious little smile.

Geoffrey strode across the room, rubbing his hands together with bogus bonhomie.

"I'm sure there's room for everything," he said. "The tree's big enough, after all. Why not have a race, see how quickly you can get it done?"

It was pathetic really, like we were going to go "oh yeah, fab idea!", and all pull together like jolly good chums. Instead, inevitably, we instantly divided into Moll and me versus Rupert. We were slightly hampered by having the sort of baubles that need cotton threading through them, whereas he had the ready-hanging sort, but we gained ground when Moll pulled off all the tinsel he'd thrown over the branches, indiscriminately and utterly at random.

It thoroughly ruffled his feathers: full marks to her for that.

"Hey!" he said, knitting his brow. "Don't do that! It's pwetty!"

"It's pwetty!" she mocked, softly. "Tin Grin likes the pwetty tinsel! Tin-sel Grin-sel!"

And she threw a strand of it at him; it draped itself over his head and caught on his glasses, at the side where the arm and the frame joined, and as he yanked at it his glasses fell off and landed on the carpet. He picked them up, his face working, ripped the tinsel off and shoved them back on his nose. A small thread of it remained, caught in the hinge, glittering golden and incongruously jolly against his face that was uncharacteristically dark with temper.

He turned to Molly and made a sudden lunge

at her; her back was turned so she didn't see him, but I thought he was going to hit her.

Oops, I thought. *Time to intervene.*

"Oi," I said, catching him by the upper arm. He tried to shake me off but I held on. His arm felt thin and bony beneath my grasp, but I could feel the tension in his muscles. "None of that."

He scowled, but turned away, and I let him go. "She started it," he muttered, childishly.

"Yeah, and I'm stopping it."

I felt the tiniest morsel of pity for him stir in me, that he'd been moved enough to respond for once instead of just standing there in his usual android-like manner, letting himself be got at. It made him slightly more human. But only very slightly.

When we finished the tree it had a Fry side and a Horton side; there wasn't a single centimetre we'd worked on together, not one branch where our respective decorations hung side by side. Mum and Geoffrey didn't comment on it – they probably didn't even notice – but as it stood there moulting steadily throughout the holidays it seemed somehow symbolic of the whole thing: Christmas, our two families, our cobbled-together lives. We shared a house and all that implied, but our lives couldn't properly be described as

161

interwoven. We were all too different for that, too individual: we had our own family traditions, our own ways of doing things. Mum and Geoffrey might have got married, but it would take more than that for our two families to knit together. And frankly, I couldn't see a time when we ever would.

Mum capitulated about the turkey, and Geoffrey cooked it as promised. It was brought to the Christmas dinner table in a state of fragrant golden perfection and accompanied by roast potatoes, Brussels sprouts, small crisp rolls of bacon-wrapped sausages, bread sauce, cranberry sauce, chestnut stuffing – the things that pub menus kitschly describe as "all the trimmings", the things that Moll and I had scarcely seen, let alone eaten, in our lives, apart from on television, and you can't smell them on television.

The smell was overwhelmingly delectable. My mouth watered, and my stomach gave a small growl of greed.

"Yum-*my*," Molly said, and her eyes gleamed. "Cor, Geoffrey, aren't you clever!"

Geoffrey allowed himself a tiny, modest little preen before saying, "I'll just go and get the pancakes."

He'd cooked those too – tiny buckwheat

162

pancakes filled with spinach and ricotta and pine nuts and covered with a sauce made of sun-dried tomatoes. The vegetarian option. He'd been out in the kitchen since seven thirty that morning, chopping and stirring and basting, and had chased Mum out when she'd poked her head round the door to see what he was up to. Not that she'd have been much help – it was obvious he was a far better cook than she'd ever be.

"It's your Christmas too," he'd said. "You go and sit down and relax."

He was clearly super-organized and efficient: he joined us for the ritual present-opening, and for coffee and biscuits (home-made) at eleven, and then at twelve thirty the kitchen door opened and in he came, apron-clad and bearing a tray upon which resided a bottle of champagne and five glasses.

"A little aperitif, Madame, *et les enfants aussi?*" He even had the cod French accent.

I could see Mum loved it all, adored being spoiled and looked after. I suppose it was all pretty impressive, really; Geoffrey was going overboard to try and make it a special occasion, fair play to him.

He came in with the dish of pancakes, and placed them with a flourish in front of Mum.

"*Et voilà!*"

Mum thanked him, took a plate from the top of the pile (carefully warmed beforehand in the bottom oven), and dug the serving spoon into the pancake dish. She looked at me, her eyebrows raised enquiringly.

"How many, Mattie?"

"Stuff that," I said. "I'm having the turkey."

OK, perhaps it was a bit abrupt. Perhaps I could have been more sensitive to Mum's vegetarian sensibilities. But honestly: the way she reacted, anyone would have thought I'd just announced I was leaving school and setting up home with an unemployed Rastafarian dope-smoker. (Come to think of it, she'd probably have been happier if I'd said that.)

Her face fell a mile. You could practically hear the thud of her jaw dropping.

"But Mattie, you can't!"

"Why not?" I said, and laughed. I think probably the laugh didn't help, but really, it was ridiculous.

"Because you're vegetarian."

"No, Mum," I said firmly. "You're vegetarian. I'm vegetarian at home a lot of the time, because there's no choice. But today, as there is a choice, I'm choosing to be a carnivore."

"Omnivore, actually," Rupert put in cleverly, with impeccable bad timing. Everyone ignored him.

164

"I see." Mum looked as if she was about to burst into tears. She turned to Molly. "Does this apply to you, too?"

"Well…" Molly hesitated, loyally. Like I said before, she's got a kinder heart than me.

"Oh, for God's sake!" I burst out, impatiently. "This is a slice of turkey we're talking about, not crack cocaine! We're not going to be damned to eternal hell because a bit of some creature's carcass passes our lips."

Mum winced slightly at that, and pressed her mouth into a thin line.

"It's all right," she said. "I'm not going to forbid you. Heaven knows, I don't want to make a fuss, not when Geoffrey's gone to so much trouble." And she spooned out a minute portion of the pancakes on to the plate and set it in front of herself.

"Thank Christ for that," I muttered, *sotto voce*, and then the rest of us all fell to passing plates of turkey and dishes of vegetables to each other, with careful emphatic good manners, while Mum sat in martyred silence in front of her doll-sized helping of pancakes and Geoffrey danced old-womanishly around us all with his bottles, filling our glasses with red or white or Coke.

"Would you like some potatoes, Mrs Fwy?" Rupert passed her the dish, politely, and she smiled at him.

"Thank you, Rupert, that's very kind of you. But listen, you really must stop calling me Mrs Fry, you know: I'm Mrs Horton now."

Rupert's face darkened, in much the same way it had when Molly had thrown the tinsel at him; even Mum, with her blithe conviction that this stepfamily thing was working just peachily, couldn't fail to notice.

"So why not just call me Alice?" she added, hastily.

Feeling vaguely guilty about the turkey episode, and more as a diversion than anything else, I asked Rupert to pass me the gravy. He obligingly reached for the jug and turned to me with it; and then, with studied deliberation, he looked me straight in the eye and dropped the gravy, jug and all, on to my lap.

I let out a shriek like a stuck pig, said an extremely rude word, and leapt to my feet.

"****!" I yelled. "You ****** ******, Rupert!"

"Mattie!" Mum intervened, looking shocked. "It was an accident!"

"Like hell it was!" I looked down at myself, at the black jeans and new black silk shirt, her Christmas present to me, that I'd dressed myself in so carefully before lunch in an attempt to make an effort. The gravy had landed mostly on my legs and was now dripping steadily on to the carpet, but it had splashed halfway up the front of the shirt, and there was a large glob of it on the right sleeve.

"It was," Rupert said, with infuriating calm. "I didn't do it on purpose."

"Yeah, right. In which case you're just a clumsy bloody idiot. Look at this shirt — it's ruined!" I wailed.

Geoffrey came dashing in from the kitchen with a tea towel, and began dabbing ineffectually at me with it.

"You might apologize, Rupert, even if it was an accident," he told his son, over his shoulder.

"Sowwy," Rupert muttered, sulkily.

"Sure you are." I pushed my chair back and warded Geoffrey off with one hand. "Don't do that, you're just making it worse. I'm going to get changed."

Mum stood up, and picked up my plate. "I'll put your dinner in the oven to keep hot."

"Don't bother: I'm not hungry any more."

I stomped off upstairs, where I put on the most un-Christmassy things I could find, a stained old pair of jogging bottoms and a huge grey misshapen sweatshirt. Then I threw myself on to my bed and plugged myself into my Walkman, turning up the volume to the point of discomfort in order to blot out the travesty of Christmas I could otherwise hear taking place in the dining room below.

After some time – I may even have dozed off – I suddenly looked up; and there, framed in the doorway like a mirage, and clutching a glass of red wine, stood Sam.

"Hi!" I sat up, and tore the headphones from my ears. "What are you doing here?"

"Come to say Merry Christmas. And give you your present." He sat down on the foot of the bed, next to me, and raised his glass. "Your stepfather gave me this. Cheers!" And he drained the glass in one long swallow.

"Oh, yeah: cheers." I looked down at myself, at my disgusting old clothes. "God, I look shocking. Some food got spilt on me, you see, so I had to get changed."

"You look pretty good to me, babe. You always do. Let me give you your present."

I felt disproportionately pleased to see him. To tell the truth, I'd recently been getting the distinct feeling that our relationship was on its way out. Sam had been calling round less and less, and I'd been caring about it pretty much the same amount. I'd been hard pushed to find the enthusiasm to buy him a Christmas present, settling eventually for a rather naff, chunky identity bracelet from the market, and I'd been neither surprised nor particularly upset when the end of term came and went with no sign of a return present from him. To be honest, I was half expecting to get the push once we were back at school.

But here he was now, taking an expensive-looking gift-wrapped object from the pocket of his denim jacket.

"What is it?" I tore off the paper excitedly, like a child, and Sam smiled.

"Hope you like it. The girl in the shop said it was – you know – classy."

It was a large bottle of perfume: Christian Dior, expensive, and undeniably classy.

"Oh, Sam!" I pulled off the cap and sprayed some on me, on my neck and wrists. "It's fab! It must have cost you a bomb."

Sam just shrugged, but I felt suddenly close to tears, ridiculously moved that he should have spent so much money on something for me that was so hopelessly romantic. I twisted myself round towards him and gave him a hug, and he hugged me back, an artlessly warm affectionate embrace without an ounce of passion. I remember thinking as we held each other that it was probably the first time we had shown genuine fondness for each other.

It was the first and last time. He reached away from me for a moment to set his empty wine glass down on the floor and to wriggle out of his jacket, then pulled me to him again, with sudden force, and we both toppled over on to the bed with Sam lying half on top of me. He began to kiss me, roughly, pulling and pushing at my clothes at the same time, and stroking and kneading the flesh he was exposing. As I kissed him back I was monitoring his hands, pushing them away from time to time as they wandered round my no-go areas, but they just kept returning to a different bit of me. It was like grappling with an octopus.

I was aware, dimly, of him managing to get my sweatshirt pushed up to my armpits; he made a small triumphant noise, deep in his throat, and all at once I just couldn't be bothered to fend him off any more. *I still fancy him,* I thought, *I* like *him touching me, it feels good. And he quite obviously likes it. Why not just let him?*

So I pulled him closer to me, wound myself round him and kissed him with a passion I'd never felt before. For a few moments I just lost myself in physical pleasure: I was aware of a strange plucking sensation, deep in my abdomen, and I realized, with a small shock of self-discovery, that it was desire. Real, grown-up, sexual desire.

Sam clearly noticed some change in me: he pushed me away, just a few centimetres, and looked into my face.

"Are you going to give me my Christmas present, then?" he whispered, and gave a wolfish little grin.

"What?" I couldn't think what he meant. "But I've already..."

Then it dawned on me. *Sex.* He wanted to make love to me, there on my bed, in the room I shared with my little sister. What a ridiculous expression that is: love was the last thing on his mind. He moved his face closer to mine so that our noses were almost touching. His eyes had almost totally changed colour, the pupils huge and black with lust.

"It's all right," he told me. "I'm fixed up."

"What?" I said again, stupidly, my mind racing. This was what all the teen mags warned about, getting into risky situations alone with a boy, going too far, going all the way... And I hadn't exactly sat there primly, had I: I'd encouraged him every step of the way.

He leant across me, reaching for the jacket he'd dropped on the carpet, and grinned again.

"It's all right. You won't get pregnant."

"No; wait."

I held on to him, thinking frantically; but he misinterpreted the action and, taking my hand, held it against the front of his trousers.

"Look what you do to me," he whispered, in my ear.

171

I could feel the hardness of him beneath the thin fabric; my mouth felt full of sand, and I could hear the pounding of blood in my ears.

And that was how Geoffrey discovered us when he came blundering in to the room. I don't know who was the more embarrassed, him or me.

"Oh, gosh," he stammered. He looked at the floor and took off his specs, wiping them on the bottom of his jumper. "Oh, my goodness – I'm so sorry. I did knock but you obviously didn't – er – I was just coming to ask if you – um—"

I leapt to my feet, adjusting my clothes frantically as I did so and almost knocking Sam out in the process.

"Just go, will you!" I screeched. "Just get out!"

"Oh, yes – um – of course – I'm, er – I'm terribly, um – oh, heavens." He pushed his glasses back on to his nose and backed clumsily from the room without looking at us.

Sam didn't appear embarrassed in the slightest. He stood up, with a heavy sigh.

"Guess I'd better go." He picked up his jacket from the floor and slung it over his shoulder. "I'll see you back at school, yeah? And maybe we'll get to finish this another time."

"Maybe."

I didn't want to look at him but couldn't seem to help myself. I was transfixed by him, by what we'd almost done, by how easy it would have been.

He crouched down beside me, and took my face between his hands so our eyes met. His were back to their normal colour, a pale cool blue.

"I hope we do," he said. "Some time soon. Because you were enjoying it as much as me, weren't you?"

I heard the heavy clump of his feet as he went downstairs, followed by the slam of the front door. What I really wanted was to stay in that bedroom for ever, never have to face anyone ever again. But I knew that was impossible, not least because Mum was calling my name up the stairs.

I went to the door, reluctantly, and threw it open.

"What?"

"Would you come down, please?"

Geoffrey must have told her. *Oh God!* How could I wriggle out of it, what could I say we were doing? Admiring my birthmark? Debating the merits of belly-button piercing?

I decided attack was the best form of defence.

"How dare you barge into my bedroom like that?" I demanded, stomping into the kitchen and glaring at Geoffrey. He went faintly pink, and Mum started to say something but I wouldn't let her. "Is it too much to ask for a bit of privacy round here? I mean, it's bad enough having to share my bedroom, but I don't expect people to just come bursting in whenever they feel like it! I suppose you've told her what you saw? Or assumed you saw," I added, as an afterthought.

Mum looked puzzled. "He hasn't told me anything. I don't know what you mean."

"No, of course you don't," I muttered sullenly.

"I haven't told her anything. Truly," Geoffrey put in, and spread his hands appeasingly.

Mum put a hand on my shoulder. "I only wanted you to come down and join in. We're about to play Trivial Pursuit. You enjoy that, don't you? You're always so good at it."

"Don't patronize me!"

"I'm not patronizing you. I only—" Mum swallowed, and took a deep breath. "Mattie darling, it's Christmas. We should all be spending it together, not with you shut away upstairs with that boy."

"He has got a name," I said, belligerently.

"Of course he has. Sam. Upstairs with Sam."

"Well, you don't have to worry," I said, "because he's gone home now."

"All right. Well look, why not come down

174

now and have a drink? And I'll make you a sandwich — you missed your lunch, you must be hungry."

She and Geoffrey exchanged looks, sending each other messages I couldn't fathom.

"Are you going to tell her?" Geoffrey prompted, gently.

"Tell me what?"

And then she told me that, while I'd been upstairs with That Boy, my father had telephoned, wanting to speak to Molly and me.

"It was all rather awkward," she said, brushing her hair distractedly from her face. "He was being difficult. I think he'd probably been drinking. He wanted to know why he hadn't heard from you, he was accusing me of not passing his letter on. Molly wouldn't come to the phone, she refused point-blank."

"But why didn't you come and get me? Why did you just assume I didn't want to speak to him either? Why do you always have to make decisions for me?"

I knew I was being unfair, but I couldn't seem to stop myself. It was as if all the events of the past few hours, the row over the turkey, the spilt gravy, the ruined silk shirt, the near miss up in my room with Sam, all of them had crystallized into a hard, unforgiving knot in the pit of my stomach.

"He hung up," Geoffrey was telling me, "he hung up before anyone could tell you."

He was only trying to be helpful, but his intervention threw me into a complete rage. I really lost it: I mean, totally. I ranted and raved like an absolute lunatic, roaring at them both about lack of privacy and trying to run my life for me, aware of my hair flying about my face and spittle spraying from my mouth. Molly came into the kitchen, drawn by the drama, and I could see her worried white face behind Geoffrey's shoulder, bobbing around as if she was drowning.

But at the same time I was also aware, in a small detached part of myself, of a curious sensation of control. Not control of myself, but of the situation: that I could say and do exactly what I wanted, and nobody would try and stop me or tell me to moderate my speech or behaviour. It gave me a sense of power over them all, coupled with an oddly perverse but very strong wish that someone would do just that, shout at me to shut up, to grow up, to take me by the shoulders and shake me and shake me until I stopped…

Eventually, I did stop. By myself. I took a long, juddering breath and held on to it. I was shaking, I could see my hands trembling on the table in front of me where I'd slammed them down to emphasize some point or other.

I let the breath out, slowly.

"If I want to speak to my father, I will." My voice was shaking, too, to match my hands. "And if I want to see him, I'll do that, as well." I walked to the kitchen door, forcing myself to take slow measured steps, not wanting to give them the satisfaction of seeing me flounce off in a stupid childish tantrum. When I reached the door I turned back to them. They were grouped around the table, gawping at me with open mouths, like goldfish.

"And I just want you to know it's been the shittiest Christmas I've ever had in my entire life."

chapter thirteen

"You're not serious," Jaz said, with a pitying look. "Didn't you tell me he used to beat your mum up?"

"Well, yes, but—"

"Yes, but nothing," she said, briskly. "He's violent, he hasn't given your mum a penny in all this time for you and your sister, you haven't heard a dicky bird from him in — what? — five years? And you're saying you're going to go and see him? You must be mad."

"I didn't say I was going to see him," I corrected her. "Not necessarily. Just maybe reply to his letter. Resume contact, that sort of thing."

Jaz gave me a long, level look. "Mad," she said again, with a decisive shake of her head. "You ask me, I reckon you're only doing it to wind your mum up."

"Yeah, well, I didn't ask you, OK?"

I was stung. I wished I hadn't told her about it now, hadn't confided in her that I was seriously considering writing to Dad and arranging to meet him when he was back in this country. Of course I wasn't doing it to wind Mum up: how could Jaz even suggest that? He was my father, when all was said and done. It sounded to me like he was regretting the past; if that was true, and he wanted to see Moll and me again, I could at least consider it. He and Mum might be divorced, but he was still my father and always would be.

Molly, however, took the same line as Jaz.

"I've already told you, I don't want to know. I don't want to write to him, I don't want to talk to him, and I certainly don't want to see him. Why are you doing this, Mattie?"

"Do you remember him?" I asked her, ignoring her question.

Molly shrugged. "A bit."

"But you were only a little kid. You were only seven. Practically a baby, really."

"Seven's not a baby. I remember enough."

"But do you remember the good bits?" There had been some of those, too: I'd been thinking about them quite a lot since Christmas. "Do you remember that time when he took us all to that Italian restaurant, you must have been about four or five? You had spaghetti bolognese and you couldn't eat it properly, you kept sucking the strands of spaghetti through your mouth, and we were all laughing. And the owner and his wife made such a fuss of us, they kept saying how pretty we were and how proud of us Mum and Dad must be."

Molly's mouth curved upwards slightly at the memory. "I remember that. Dad called us his bambini for ages afterwards."

"And how about that summer when we went camping in the south of France? We drove around from place to place and pitched our tent in different sites for a couple of nights each."

"Was that when it was so hot all the time?"

"Yeah – Dad kept taking us on the beach at night, when it was cooler. We had those barbecues, do you remember?"

The evocative mixed smells of grilled meat, charcoal and suncream...

"And Mum and Dad always had those great big jugs of red wine, do you remember those? And Dad took us to hotels for breakfast every morning and bought us hot chocolate and rolls."

Until that moment I had forgotten all about it, but suddenly I could taste the hot chocolate, thick and sweet in my mouth. It was served not in cups but bowls, large rough china ones like cereal bowls.

Molly's face took on a distant, far-away look as she remembered some more – the good happy memories of our past life that had become obliterated with time and the bitterness of Mum and Dad's parting and their divorce.

"And that night when Mum kept saying it was going to rain and Dad insisted it wasn't, and there was that massive thunderstorm and you and I were running around in our swimsuits with Dad in the pouring rain, just to get cool," Molly said.

"And Mum was cowering inside the tent getting all hot and bothered, and Dad kept teasing her about her inner poise."

The memory of it came back to me, sharply, overlaying the dreamy recollections of the good times with a sense of cold hard realism. *Where's your inner poise now, Alice, he'd taunted her. Is the thunder messing with your headspace?* He'd had no time for her hippy-dippy ways, they'd driven him berserk, and he'd never lost any opportunity to have a dig at her. But he'd also known she was terrified of thunderstorms, and instead of reassuring and comforting her he'd been cavorting out in the rain with Moll and me. At the time I'd thought nothing of it, but now the uncomfortable thought came to me that teasing Mum about her fear had been unkind, if not downright cruel.

It's all in the past now. I shook my head, like a dog emerging from water, to clear my thoughts. *It's all in the past.* And anyway, that was with Mum. He was never like that with Molly and me. We didn't see that much of him, but when he was home on leave he was always nice to us. Always. *Except that time he hit me...*

"So are you going to see him then, or what?"

Molly's voice was cool, uninterested. She wasn't swayed by reminiscences of happy moments, nor would she be. She had made up her mind and would stick to it. Not like me. The truth was, I couldn't think what I wanted to do, and remembering that awful moment when his hard fist had made contact with the soft yielding flesh of my face wasn't helpful at all. *It was a one-off. He didn't mean it, I'm certain he didn't. He's probably never forgiven himself.*

"I don't know. I'm still thinking about it. But don't tell Mum, OK? It's my decision, and I don't want her sticking her nose in."

Molly lifted a shoulder. "It's up to you. I won't tell Mum. But I think you're mad. The happy memories don't make up for the awful things that went on; you shouldn't let them."

Why was everyone so keen to tell me I was mad? I wasn't a child, unable to discern the difference between right and wrong, good and evil. If I decided to see Dad again – *if* – it would be entirely my decision. It was a situation only I could control: and it felt good to have at least one thing in my life I could say that about.

Sam started laying siege to me as soon as we went back to school after Christmas. The first day back, he sidled up to me in the corridor.

"Hiya, babe." He put his arm around my waist and his tongue in my ear. "When are we going to get it together again?"

"Put her down, Sam. Take your mind off lovebites and get it on to megabytes."

It was Andy Cooper, strolling down the corridor with a crowd of other sixth-form trendies. The girl behind him, a pretty, vaguely familiar girl with blonde hair that swung about her face like a bell, smiled felinely.

"What's he on about?" I asked Sam.

"Computer Studies. Pearson's always on at me for being late, but hey – who cares? I'd rather be with you."

"Come on, Sammy," said the blonde. "You don't want to get on Mr Pearson's wrong side again. We'd better go."

She had an irritating, little-girly voice. She took Sam firmly by the arm and literally pulled him away from me. You could practically hear the pop of suction as we disengaged. I watched as she marched him down the corridor, and just as they rounded the corner, I saw him sneak an arm behind her and put his hand on her backside. A shaft of jealousy shot through me, but I told myself not to be so stupid. *It's just Sam. He's always like that with girls.*

"You all right, then?"

I turned round: Andy was still standing there, watching me watching Sam and Blondie.

"Shouldn't I be?" I snapped.

Andy raised an eyebrow. "OK, OK. Don't get out of your pram, I was only asking. Just wondered if you minded seeing your boyfriend groping another girl's bum."

"He was hardly groping her. He was just being Sam. Or should I say Sammy," I added, imitating Blondie's eight-year-old's intonation.

He smiled, a tight humourless little grimace. "Yeah, right. He just can't help himself, can he?"

"Look, Andy, what's your problem? It doesn't bother me — why should it bother you?" A sudden thought struck me. "You're not jealous, are you?"

"Jealous?" He looked alarmed. "Why should I be jealous?"

"Because Sam gets all the girls, and you—"

"And I don't," he finished, bitterly. "Gee, thanks."

"I didn't mean that. Don't get in a huff."

But I had meant it, and we both knew it. I

didn't blame Andy for being offended; he was popular and had girlfriends, I'd seen him with them. But he wasn't in the same league as Sam. Sam's girls (with the notable exception of me) were always sexy, glamorous creatures, whereas Andy's were just – well, just girls, I suppose.

He regarded me, levelly and at length. "Be careful," he said at last.

"What?" It seemed an odd kind of thing to say. "Careful of what?"

"Don't let him—" He stopped, mid-sentence, and pulled a face. "Just be careful, that's all. I mean it."

I told Sam about it, a couple of days later. It was after school and we were up in my room, rediscovering each other after the cooling-off of last term.

"Oh, he's just jealous," he said airily, pulling me towards him.

"That's what I thought. In fact, it's what I told him." Slight fib, but so what?

"Did you?" He drew himself back and looked at me with interest. "You told him he was jealous? And what did he say?"

"Nothing much," I shrugged. "That's when he told me to be careful."

"Yeah, you said. Prat."

"I thought you were supposed to be mates?"

"We are mates. Trouble with Andy is, he's always been jealous of me. Like you said."

"Why?"

"Isn't it obvious? I'm better at sport than him, cleverer than him, better-looking." *More modest*, I thought, but decided not to say it. "And I get all the funky chicks, while he's left with the dogs. He's a total div."

He grinned at me, a smug, self-satisfied grin, and I felt a sudden unpleasant spurt of dislike for him. How could he be so mean about his best mate? I couldn't imagine me saying the same about Jaz, comparing her so unfavourably to me. And I wasn't sure about being called a funky chick, either.

But then he started kissing me again, and all my negative thoughts flew right out of the window. He pulled my top up and undid my bra and, despite the warning bells clanging in my brain, I let him. I didn't even attempt to monitor his hands this time, I just let him do what he wanted.

"God," he murmured admiringly. "You really are up for it, aren't you?"

I heard a sudden noise, outside on the landing, and pushed him away. "Ssshh!"

A look of annoyance crossed his face. "What? What are you playing at, Mattie? You can't just lead me on like that and then——"

186

"Sssshh!" I hissed again, urgently. "There's someone out there!"

I nodded in the direction of the bedroom door and then, in one quick movement, pulled my jumper down, slid off the bed, crossed the floor and flung open the door.

Rupert stood there, right in the doorway, slightly hunched over. He straightened up guiltily, caught out.

"What do you think you're playing at?" I demanded. "You were eavesdropping, weren't you?"

"No I wasn't, I was just—"

"Yes you were, you little pervert!"

Sam came to stand behind me, his tall, sport-developed body almost filling the door frame.

"What's going on?" His voice was deep and full of authority, and I realized that to Rupert he seemed like an adult, a grown man.

A look of fear passed across Rupert's face, and he said, "Nothing – nothing!" He turned to me, appealing. "Your mum just asked me to see if you wanted a cup of tea. I wasn't eaves-dwopping – honestly!"

Sam took a step forward, and wagged a stern finger under Rupert's nose.

"You better not have been listening in, my son. Because you know what happens to little

187

eavesdroppers, don't you?" Rupert shook his head, mesmerized. "Their ears drop off!" Sam said triumphantly. "Or even other, more painful bits of their anatomy," he added, feebly.

Oh, well done Sam, I thought, with exasperation. Why couldn't he just have said he'd do Rupert over if he caught him earwigging again, instead of talking to him as if he was about four years old?

The look of terror literally fell away from Rupert's face, and was replaced by his normal expression of smug disdain.

"Oh, wight," he said, lifting his chin the better to look down his nose at us. "I'll bear that in mind. I certainly wouldn't want my ears to dwop off. I'll tell your mother tea isn't wequired, shall I?"

He turned on his heel and went snootily downstairs without waiting for an answer, and Sam made a lunge at him, as if to stop him, but I put my hand on his arm.

"Leave him," I told him wearily. "He's not worth it. He's just a pain."

"Too right he's a pain – how can you put up with living in the same house as him? He's a real – what's the expression? A cuckoo in the woodpile."

"Don't you mean cuckoo in the nest?"

The tiniest flicker of annoyance crossed

Sam's features. "Whatever. Right then; where were we?"

He put his arms around my waist and made to draw me back into the bedroom, pulling the door shut behind us with one foot.

"Hang on," I told him.

Another flicker of annoyance, more noticeable this time. "What d'you mean, hang on? You were all over me just now. You can't blow hot and cold like this, Mattie – you'll get a reputation."

"A reputation?" I stared at him. "What kind of reputation?"

He muttered something under his breath.

"What?" I demanded. "What did you say?"

"A prick-tease," he said, loudly. "Is that what you want people to call you?"

"Of course not."

I moved into the room and closed the door behind us, my mind in a spin. Part of me – a small cold angry part – wanted to ask him how he thought I would get that kind of reputation unless he spread it around. But beneath my anger a little voice was crying, *Don't! Don't argue with him! Don't wind him up! You'll lose him!*

Then Sam smiled at me, a slow beguiling smile, and he put out a hand and touched my cheek in that tender way of his that always made me melt.

"It's OK," he said. "I know exactly what the problem is. It's being in this house, isn't it? You can't relax if you think your sister or your stepfather or whoever might come bursting in at any moment."

I nodded: it wasn't totally that, but it seemed easier just to agree with him.

"No worries," Sam went on. "It was stupid of me not to realize before."

What could I say? I kept my mouth shut.

"Well, it just so happens," his eyes gleamed, "that I know just the place. It's warm, it's dry, it's cosy, and I can absolutely guarantee we won't be disturbed. It's the perfect place to – you know – get it on."

I frowned. "Where is it? Not the cave?"

"No, not the cave!" He laughed, and tapped the side of his nose with his finger. "You'll have to wait and see."

"But I can't go anywhere now – Mum's expecting me to be in for tea, and then there's homework and stuff," I gabbled. I felt backed into a corner, trapped.

"It's OK," Sam said again. "It's too late to go tonight. There's plenty of time – just so long as I know you're serious about this, and not just stringing me along. You are serious, aren't you, Mattie?"

Was I serious about him? I didn't know. Just

before Christmas I'd have said no; I'd thought we were drifting apart, and hadn't been especially bothered about it. But now: now I felt different. The truth was, I couldn't resist him. He incited feelings in me I'd never experienced before, excitement and danger and passion. It was the passion that was irresistible; it, and he, made me weak at the knees.

"Mattie?"

He looked at me, and I looked at him, and the look went on for a very long time, until: "Yes," I whispered, eventually. I couldn't bear the thought of saying no; I knew what would happen – goodbye, Sam.

"Good," he whispered back. "Because you know what? I'm serious about you, too. Very serious. I've never felt like this about anybody before. The thing is, I think I'm in love with you."

I wanted to say I loved him too: I knew it was what he wanted to hear, what he expected even, but I just couldn't. I had the curious sensation of falling, spiralling downwards, dizzily losing control of the situation, as well as my limbs and my senses, and then Sam leant forwards and kissed me and all I could think of was the feel of his soft warm lips on mine.

chapter fourteen

Writing to my father was easier than I'd imagined. I'd intended just to send a short note, telling him that I would be happy to see him when he was back. But instead I found myself writing a real epistle, pages and pages of flimsy blue airmail paper in which I found myself, rather to my surprise, pouring out my heart about all kinds of things: Molly's unequivocal refusal to have anything to do with him, Mum and Geoffrey's marriage, Sam, and of course, Rupert.

We call him Tin Grin, I wrote. *Do you think that's mean of us? Mum says it is. But really, Dad, if you met him you'd understand. He's everybody's idea of the horrible, infuriating, irritating little brother none of the grown-ups will hear a word against, only of course he isn't our brother. We don't even have that blood tie that, in time, when he's older and (possibly, though I doubt it) less objectionable, might bind us together like proper siblings and make us forget the awfulness of our relationship when we were growing up.*

When I read that bit back I had a moment of

doubt, a pinprick of panic that Dad might read between the lines, as it were, and think I was talking not about me and Rupert, but about me and himself. After all, what I had said, the last bit about blood ties, could equally well apply to us. Would he think I was trying to make him feel guilty? And if so, would he decide against seeing me again after all? I didn't think I could bear that, not having come up against so much opposition before making up my mind to contact him.

Then I realized I was fed up with trying to second guess other people's reactions to things. How could I possibly tell what was going through people's minds? I couldn't even keep up with what was going through my own, half the time.

If Dad takes offence, that's his problem, not mine, I told myself firmly, and stuffed the letter in the envelope and sealed and addressed it before I changed my mind. *There. Now I'll just have to wait and see.*

Mum's response, when I told her, wasn't at all what I'd imagined. I'd thought she would either a) go ballistic or b) go hysterical, but to my surprise she did neither.

"Oh," she said.

It was over supper one evening; she calmly

reached for the water jug, buttered a roll, and then carried on eating.

I blinked. "Is that all? *Oh?*"

"What do you want me to say?" She put a forkful of bean casserole into her mouth, and smiled. "He's your father, Mattie. I'm not going to forbid you."

Just like you didn't forbid me to eat the turkey at Christmas, I thought, and felt an irrational gush of annoyance at her apparent impartiality.

"You might show an interest," I complained.

"Darling, I am interested. It's just—"

"Just what?"

"I just wonder about your motivation."

"My motivation?" It was almost the reaction I'd had from Jaz when I'd told her. "What d'you mean, my motivation?"

"I suppose I wonder why you're so keen to see Dad now, when for years you swore you'd never want him in your life again. I'm not saying that's the right way to feel: simply that it's very different from what you're saying now."

If you ask me, you're only doing it to wind your mum up...

"I'm not keen to see him. Not necessarily. Did I say I was keen to see him?" I could hear my voice rising in both pitch and volume, and struggled to control it.

"No, you didn't. You just said you'd written to him."

"Exactly. I just said I'd written to him. That's all. One poxy little letter, in nearly six years. Not really much to make a song and dance about, is it?"

I looked round the table at the others, appealing to them to back me up. Rupert wasn't there, he'd gone to Michael's for tea; but Molly just glared at me, the words *Shut Up* clearly visible above her head (she hates a scene, does Moll), and Geoffrey opened his mouth to say something, then obviously thought better of it and shut it again.

I pounced on him.

"Geoffrey," I demanded. "What do you think? Do you think it's a terrible crime to write back to my father, having had his letter in my drawer for four months?"

"I don't think it's a crime, no."

"Oh, good. Geoffrey doesn't think it's a crime. So tell me, Geoffrey." I put my elbows on the table and leant towards him, matily. "Tell me what you do think."

Geoffrey regarded me calmly for a few moments. The resemblance between him and his son had never been stronger, and the dislike I felt for him at that moment had never been more intense.

"What I think," he said, without emphasis, "is that it's nothing to do with me. Or your mother, or anyone else. I think it should be entirely your decision."

I felt curiously let down, as if I'd wanted Geoffrey to rant like the Wicked Stepfather and tell me what a selfish little cow I was being, and how upset I was making my mother. Ridiculous, isn't it? For a start, Geoffrey couldn't rant his way out of a cake tin, and for a second, if he'd tried I'd have ripped his arms off and hit him over the head with the mucky end. That's not what stopped him, though. He was just a naturally reasonable man. And that – *that* – is precisely what riled me. I didn't want people to be reasonable with me. I wanted them to yell and scream at me so I could feel justified in yelling and screaming back. The stupid thing was, I couldn't for the life of me work out why I so badly wanted to yell and scream.

Mum said, "Mattie," and put her hand over mine. "I accept that you want to have contact with your father again. I do understand. We all do."

"I don't," Molly put in, staunchly, but not expecting to be taken notice of.

"You're his daughter. The bond between parent and child is very strong. We do understand, Mattie. I promise you. After all, we're parents ourselves, Geoffrey and I."

They exchanged glances, over the table, and something about the way they looked at each other, at the same time lovey-dovey and self-satisfied, set off warning bells in my head.

"Oh God," I said, in disgust. "You're not pregnant, are you?"

Molly made a strange little choking sound, part amusement, part embarrassment, part horror, and I realized the stupidity of what I'd said.

"But you couldn't be, could you? I forgot. You're far too old."

"I'm not, actually," Mum said, quickly. "But no, I'm not pregnant."

She didn't look at all shocked at the suggestion; in fact, she looked rather wistful, as if the idea appealed. It appalled me, I'm telling you.

"Thank God for that," I said, with heat. "Just imagine; the thought of another Rupert."

I didn't mean to be bitchy, I really didn't: it just kind of slipped out. But Mum took a sudden inward breath, as if I'd slapped her. Then she put her fork down on her plate of food, with sudden deliberation, and leant back in her chair.

"Mattie," she said, carefully, "you have a very

unkind tongue," and there were tears in her eyes.

"What? What did I say?"

I couldn't understand what I'd said that was so terrible. I mean, she knew how I felt about Rupert. It was hardly a state secret. And Geoffrey must have had some idea. It was impossible to have lived in our house for the past however-long-it-was and think everything was just fine and dandy between us.

I turned to him again. "What did I say?" I asked him, expecting him to smooth things over in his usual bland fashion. But to my surprise, his mouth was set and he wouldn't meet my eye. It was the nearest I'd ever seen him come to looking angry. He got up from the table and went across to Mum, patting her shoulder solicitously.

"Are you all right?"

She sniffed, and placed her hand over his, nodding and giving him a watery little smile. "Yes, darling. Are you?"

"Me?" Geoffrey laughed shortly. "Why shouldn't I be?"

"Oh for Christ's sake!" I growled. Why was everybody ignoring me all of a sudden? "Why's everybody getting so heavy? I was only joking. I didn't mean to upset anybody. Mum?"

I turned to her, appealing, but she just shook

her head and dabbed at her nose with a hanky in a martyred way, and wouldn't say anything.

"Oh well, if you're going to get all emotional," I said grouchily. "I'm off. I've got homework to do."

Upstairs, the door to Rupert's room was, unusually, wide open. He normally kept it shut tight, day and night, only opening it enough to slide in and out, as if he was making a nuclear reactor in there and didn't want to be found out. I remembered him coming back in a rush on his way out to Michael's, muttering something about having forgotten some computer game or other. He must have left the door open in his haste.

Computer. I stood on the threshold of his room, experimentally, and craned my neck to peer round the door. Yup. There it was, his computer, sitting temptingly on his desk, the geometric pattern of the screen saver whirling dizzily around. I hadn't been able to catch up on the adventures of Ty'n Grhyn since that first time: I'd wanted to, driven by a mixture of righteous indignation and plain nosiness, but Rupert had been around rather a lot and sneaking into his bedroom when he was downstairs watching TV was just too risky.

But now he was out, and wouldn't be back for some time, judging by previous occasions

he'd been to Michael's. I tiptoed into his room,
shut the door behind me, and sat down in front
of the screen.

In which the Mighty Ty'n Grhyn thwarts the Bitch-Queen and her Cohort Sa'am.

"o Sa'am" murmed M'Atil Da'aa
"kiss me again your so hansome..."
"But no" Sa'am responded "we must
ready ourselves for the battle with
the Mighty Ty'n Grhyn, you know how
strong and fearless he is, we musnt
wast time canodling but prepare our
selves and our troops for the
fight!
The Bitch-Queen looked at Sa'am
with aproval, he looks just like a
Greek God she thought, hes really
fit, all the girls fancy him and
I'm the one he's choosen to be
with.
(The following section is written
by Michael Phillip Stewart, aged
13, of 6 Fore St, Luscombe, Devon.)
"Away with you, wench!" Sa'am
cried, flinging the Bitch-Queen
aside. "Do not dally with me
further! I must save my strength

200

for the ensuing battle with the
Hero Warrior; in truth, I fear for
my life, for there is none mightier
than him. You must face facts, my
dear — you may lose me."
His words filled M'Atil Da'aa with
fear and trembling. She was deeply,
madly in love with Sa'am, she had
never known anyone quite like him.
Every time he kissed her he made
her heart beat so fast she thought
she might faint with ecstasy.

I'd read quite enough. I was so angry, it took
all my will power to exit from the document
and leave Rupert's room quietly, without
banging the door shut behind me in temper. I
went into the bathroom and locked the door,
knowing I'd get at least a few undisturbed
minutes in there.

The little ratbags! Not only Rupert, but
Michael too! It wasn't just that, though – the
thing that really made me furious was they'd
quite obviously been reading my diary. That
thing about looking like a Greek God and all
the girls fancying him but having chosen me:
the bit about being deeply, madly in love with
him, and fainting with ecstasy because of the
speed of my heartbeat – I'd written all of that

only a week or two ago. They'd obviously waited until I wasn't around, and then sneaked in to my room and read my diary, all the personal and intimate things I'd never shared with a living soul...

I sat down heavily on the side of the bath, hot with fury and horror and embarrassment. I could just imagine them, leafing furtively through my diary and tittering in that stupid, nudge-nudge way boys have. I started to wonder what else they might have read. Had they found the bits where I'd catalogued, in glorious Technicolor detail, exactly what we got up to when we were up in my room "revising"? Had they read the entry for Christmas Day? Had they read...?

Oh God! I put my head in my hands. It was just too awful for words. It did occur to me, just for a second, that I too had been sneaking around, reading somebody else's stuff, but I dismissed the thought instantly. It wasn't the same thing at all. My diary was private and personal; you couldn't compare it with Rupert's puerile fantasy drivel, the very thought was ridiculous. It was clear I was going to have to do three things: 1) Find a better hiding place for my diary, 2) Hack into the Adventures of Ty'n Grhyn one last time and erase it all, to destroy the evidence of my real-life adventures with

Sam, and most importantly 3) Get even with Rupert.

Jaz was beside herself when I told her.

"What?" she spluttered. "They read your diary?"

Even Jaz hadn't been privy to my diary — well, only the odd entry, carefully edited when I knew there was a chance she might ask for a sneaky peeky.

"I know," I said, grimly. "Don't worry: I'm plotting my revenge."

"But your *diary*! Some things are sacred."

"Tell me about it. They even pinched some of it to write in their poxy fantasy story — confidential things I'd written about Sam. *Intimate* things," I added.

"When you say intimate things—?"

"Oh, come on, Jaz! You know what I mean."

She eyed me beadily. "I hope I don't."

"Oh, pack it in. You sound like my mother."

"No I don't. Your mother never says things like that to you. Perhaps it would be better if she did."

"Meaning?" I glared at her, not at all liking the turn this conversation was taking.

Jaz carried on eyeing me for a second or two, then she gave a little sigh and spread her hands appeasingly, palms downwards.

"Mattie, I don't want to preach at you."

"But you're going to, anyway."

"No I'm not. Not preach. Just a – I don't know – a friendly word."

"Why do I think I'm not going to like what you've got to say?"

"Like it or not, I'm going to say it anyway."

I had a sudden childish urge to stick my fingers in my ears and hum loudly, to blot out Jaz's words. But I didn't. I stood there, and listened.

"Have you heard the rumour that's going round school? About you and Sam?"

I sighed, with exaggerated patience. "Surprise me."

She looked suddenly embarrassed, and that did surprise me. "Well…"

"For God's sake, Jaz! Cut to the chase, will you!"

"It's all round school," she said, lifting her chin, "that you and Sam are – you know – sleeping together."

I couldn't have been more shocked if she'd said we'd eloped in the holidays and I was now Mrs Barker.

"What!" I was aghast. "How on earth – who—"

"Not that I believe it," she assured me, hastily. "I just thought you ought to know, that's all."

"Oh my God!" I put my hands up to my face in horror. "Who on earth started that?"

"Isn't it obvious? Sam, of course." She spat his name out, scathingly. "It makes him out to be a big stud, in his mates' eyes at any rate."

"No, he wouldn't. He *wouldn't*," I insisted, seeing her disbelieving face. Why should he? Afterwards, maybe. If there was an afterwards. But not when I was so clearly on the verge of agreeing to it, or so he believed. What would he stand to gain? It would most likely frighten me off.

"He wouldn't," I said again.

"Wouldn't he? So who spread the same rumour about him and Vanessa, then, back in the summer?"

I was baffled. "Who's Vanessa?"

"Mattie," she said, pityingly. "You know Vanessa. Upper Sixth, blonde hair in a bob, squeaky voice?"

Blondie. I could hear her now – "*Come on, Sammy*."

"So how come I never got to hear that rumour, then?" I challenged her.

"You must have. Everybody did. It was the hot gossip of the summer holidays. Look, I told you myself – I remember."

Somewhere, in the dim and distant recesses of my memory, I recalled Jaz saying something about hot gossip. It must have been about the time of the wedding; about the time Sam asked me out that first time, when we'd gone up to the Smug's for a coffee and then he'd taken me to the cave for a snog. *Aeons ago*... I couldn't recall Jaz ever telling me what the hot gossip in question was, though.

"You never told me," I said, definitely. "I'd have remembered."

Jaz clicked her tongue. "Mattie, you've been so distracted lately I reckon you wouldn't remember if I told you I'd had a sex change."

"But this was about Sam. I'd have remembered," I repeated. "Anyway," I went on slowly, the thought just dawning on me, "why haven't you said anything about it since? You know Sam and me are an item — why didn't you tell me before about him and *Vanessa*?" I spat it out, but Jaz seemed quite unbothered. She just shrugged.

"Far as I could see, she was just another one of his many women. C'mon, Mattie — you know what he's like for sniffing around anyone with a pulse who's remotely presentable. You've seen him." I couldn't deny it. "Anyway," she went on, "it all died a death, didn't it? Vanessa didn't want anything more to do with Sam after the holidays, apparently. Once she found out what he'd been telling everyone about her. That's what the goss was, anyway." She looked hard at me. "Look, Mattie, don't blame me if you didn't hear. I wasn't about to slag your precious Sam off to you, was I? Not when I could see how you were feeling about him. And especially not once the whole Sam/Vanessa thing had blown over anyway."

"So why're you telling me now?" I asked her, suspiciously.

"Because of the rumour that's now going round about you and him," she said, slowly, as if explaining to a rather dim-witted child. "The thing is, back in the summer, Sam managed to persuade Vanessa that it wasn't him who'd started it. Just so they'd get back together. Which as we all know, they have."

"Get back together? How d'you mean?" I frowned.

"I mean get back together — as in going out together."

Now I knew she'd lost it. "Jaz," I said, mock-patiently. "I'm going out with Sam. Me. Not Vanessa. Me."

But Jaz shook her head firmly. "No, Mat. You're staying in with him. You told me so yourself. You go up to your bedroom and—"

"I haven't slept with him," I interrupted, fiercely.

"I know you haven't. I believe you. But the

trouble is, Sam's telling everybody that you have. He's spreading it around – God, Mattie, I hate telling you this, but if I don't someone else will – he's spreading it around that that's what you do together, a couple of times a week. And in the meantime, he's hanging out round school with Vanessa, and everyone can see they're a couple. I thought you knew – I thought you were ignoring it, rising above it, kind of thing. He's making a fool out of you. And her too, if you ask me," she added, in an undertone.

"Oh, is he!" I turned on her, furious. "Is he, now! Well, how come I haven't seen them 'hanging out' together, as you call it?" *But you have*, a little voice whispered in my ear. I ignored it, too full of righteous indignation to be reasonable. "And for your information, I don't believe you. I don't believe Sam would make up such a thing. We've got a really good relationship – he even told me the other day he was in love with me!"

"So who would make it up, then?"

"I don't know!" I was yelling now. "How do I know? It could be anybody! It could be…" I cast wildly around for a name. "Andy Cooper! It could easily be Andy Cooper. Or it could even be you. How do I know?"

"It wasn't me," Jaz said, quietly.

"Oh, do me a favour, Jaz, will you? You've never liked Sam."

"That's not true," she said, calmly.

"Yes, it is! How do I know you're telling the truth now, about him and this Vanessa? It could be just a pack of lies to try and put me off him."

"It isn't."

"Yeah, well, I've only got your word for that, haven't I?" I glared at her, and she looked back at me, calmly, but with pity in her eyes. It was the pity that did it.

"Just butt out, will you?" I shouted again. "Leave me and Sam alone. Just leave us alone!"

chapter fifteen

My plan for revenge on Rupert was quite simple. I intended to kidnap his precious rat, Colin. I don't mean hold him to ransom or anything ridiculous like that; just let him go missing for a day or so, to make Rupert worry and, eventually, to realize I wasn't someone to be messed with.

It was all very humane, I mean I'm not into cruelty to animals (I'm half-vegetarian, for goodness sake) — if you can call a rat an animal, that is, which is debatable. I borrowed an old aquarium from Jaz's brother Surjit, who has a serious tropical-fish habit and is always upgrading their homes. I even went to the pet shop in Luscombe and bought some bedding and food and a dish and one of those water bottle thingies. Out of my own money, too — just how cruel is that?

The hard part was putting the plan into action. I had to smuggle all the bits and pieces into the cottage, find a suitable hiding place for them, and then wait for the right moment: when Rupert went out for long enough to *accompli* the *fait*, so to speak, at a time when nobody else was around much. In the end it happened one Saturday, when Rupert and Michael were crabbing down at the cove, Mum and Geoffrey were doing the usual thrilling supermarket run, and Molly was – God knows where. Not indoors, at any rate.

The worst bit was getting the rat out of the cage and into its new temporary home. It gave me the shivers for days beforehand, just thinking about it. In the end I got the aquarium all ready and then, with gritted teeth, tipped the rat from the cage into an old shoebox (the scrabbling of its claws on the cardboard was awful) and from there into the aquarium. I slammed the lid on, tight, and held it down. I was shaking.

I sat there on Rupert's bedroom floor for ages, my jaws clamped together, clinging on to the lid of the aquarium for dear life. Then I realized I couldn't hang about for much longer; I might be discovered, caught out, and my plans to get even would go up in smoke.

I let go of the lid, gingerly, and peered cautiously through the aquarium's clear perspex side. I couldn't see any trace of the rat itself, but the turbulent state of the straw bedding indicated where it was hiding. I managed to lug the aquarium, contents and all, downstairs and out to one of the old stone outhouses that line the side of our garden, where I hid it behind a pile of old grain sacks and a rusty, broken-spoked bicycle, all of which had been there since we moved in and were hardly likely to be disturbed now.

"Welcome to your new abode," I said, with grim satisfaction. "I hope you're very happy here."

I was, to coin a phrase, on tenterhooks for the rest of the day. (I've always wondered what tenterhooks are, exactly, and how they differ from other kinds of hooks. Perhaps I need to get out more.) Mum and Geoffrey duly arrived back home, and spent the next riveting half-hour unpacking the shopping and bickering mildly about just who had forgotten to buy the puy lentils. Rupert and Michael and Molly came wandering back from their respective morning's pursuits, and somehow Michael managed to get himself invited for lunch.

As we all sat crammed round the table, I couldn't stop myself watching the pair of them as they sat together, deep in some private joke or another. *Yeah*, I thought to myself, *you two think you're just so clever, don't you? Well, M'Atil Da'aa has got a little surprise waiting for you upstairs, Ty'n Grhyn my son. Vengeance is mine, saith the Bitch-Queen.*

Geoffrey sat himself in front of the bread-board and sawed huge doorstep slices off the loaf. Then he put the knife down, cleared his throat, and looked round expectantly at us all. It was obviously announcement time.

"Now we're all here," he began. "I've got a piece of good news I'd like to share with you."

Good grief, I thought, *he's even beginning to talk like Mum now. Spooky, or what?*

"I hope you don't mind being included in the family news, Michael? The thing is, we're not often here all at the same time, and I don't think I can wait any longer to tell them." The poor lad just looked down at his plate, dead embarrassed at being singled out for attention.

"The thing is—" Geoffrey reached for Mum's hand, beaming with pride. "The thing is, I've been asked by a very prestigious American university to go and do a lecture tour there."

"It's a real honour," Mum put in. "The Dean of Faculty here is just bursting with excitement about it, he says it reflects incredibly well on both Geoffrey and the department."

"Far out," I said, drily, and reached for some bread.

Molly kicked me under the table, for some

reason. "That's brilliant; well done, Geoffrey," she said, and it's funny but I couldn't detect a trace of irony in her voice.

"What do you think, Rupert, old son? Isn't it good news?"

Rupert looked up from the tablecloth, where he had been tracing patterns with his fork. "When?" he asked, dully. "When are you going?"

He looked pastier than ever; his eyes were expressionless black pools behind his specs. His hair needed cutting and a tuft of it was sticking up from his crown in a greasy cowlick. He had a new crop of spots across his chin. I reflected that I had never seen anybody so completely and utterly unwholesome-looking.

"Easter," Geoffrey replied, eagerly. "It's for three weeks over the Easter vacation, so not long now. What do you think?" Rupert just shrugged, and fell to digging his runnels in the cloth again with the tines of his fork. I could see from Geoffrey's face that this wasn't quite the reaction he had been hoping for, that he was disappointed, but fortunately the telephone rang at that point. Mum got up to answer it, which spared us all the spectacle of her doing her Super Stepmother impression and forcing Rupert into sharing his feelings with us.

She came back into the room almost immediately, her face grave.

"It's for you, Mattie," she said.

Sam, I thought, *making arrangements for this evening*. I went into the hallway and picked up the receiver.

"Hello?"

"Is that you, Matilda?"

It was a male voice, all right, deep and gruff and faintly familiar, but it wasn't Sam's.

"Yes. Who is this?"

"It's your father, Mat. It's Dad."

I dropped the phone: literally. It fell from my grasp and on to the seagrass matting where it lay, emitting faint squeaks and squawks.

I picked it up. I was shaking, in much the same way I had been earlier when tipping Colin the rat into the aquarium.

"Hello, Dad," I breathed.

"Oh, you are there! For a moment, I thought you'd hung up."

Considering my letter to him had been such an outpouring, I had remarkably little to say to him. In fact, I could barely think of a thing to say. But it scarcely seemed to matter, as he had enough to say for both of us. After a bit, I sat down on the bottom stair and cradled the receiver between my chin and shoulder, listening to the most important and significant male voice of my childhood and making the odd agreeing noise in response.

215

"Well," he said, at last. "Now you know what I've been doing, how about filling me in on what you're up to these days?"

"Oh, this and that." I picked at a loose bit of seagrass on the stairs, feeling suddenly, ridiculously shy.

"How's school? You must be coming up for those O level things in a year or two. What is it they call them now? GCSEs."

"This year. They start next term."

"Never! So you're – what – sixteen now."

"Next month." Surely he remembered when my birthday was?

Sweet sixteen and never been kissed. The thought, from God alone knew where, drifted across my subconscious. It couldn't have been less appropriate. *The age of consent...* I thought of Sam, and the rumour Jaz said he'd spread about him and me, and felt myself blushing.

"Well well," he chuckled. "My little Mattie, all grown up. I bet you've got all the boys after you, eh?"

It was as if he'd read my mind. I felt the blush grow deeper.

"Not exactly."

"And how's the stepfamily, then? Tin Grin still getting on your nerves?"

How could I tell him that it was much, much more than simply getting on my nerves? That

Rupert was the embodiment of the thorn in my flesh, the epitome of the albatross around one's neck, the cross I had to bear made manifest. The clichés thronged my brain, but all I could manage to say was a feeble "I guess."

"And guess what? You've got another step-family, too!"

"Sorry?" For a moment I couldn't think what he meant.

"I'm married again. And I've got two children, a boy and a girl. They'll be your half-brother and -sister, I suppose." There was a pause. "Would you like to meet them?" he asked, cautiously.

"What are their names?"

"Rosie. My wife's called Rosie. And the kids are Toby and Zinnia."

Toby and Zinnia. They seemed very grand names, and quite at odds with the memories I had of my father as a rough-and-ready, beer-drinking man, a man who liked nothing better when he was home than going down the pub with his mates and coming home roaring drunk and fighting mad.

"How old are they?"

"Four and two." His voice swelled with pride for his new family.

"When are you coming back to England, then?"

"Oh, I'm back already. Didn't I tell you? The contract in Kuwait came to an end a couple of months ago, so I'm back at the ranch with Rosie and the kids. Your letter was forwarded here."

"So where's the ranch?"

"Surrey. Near Guildford. It's great, Mattie. It's like a mansion. We've got a big garden for the kids, with a swimming pool and everything. Not that we get much chance to use it with the weather we have in this country."

"Not like in Kuwait."

"Aye, you're right there."

There was another pause, a longer one this time.

"Are you rich?" I asked him, eventually.

He gave an embarrassed little laugh. "I s'pose I am. Richer than what I used to be, for sure."

Not a penny in all this time for you and your sister — not a dicky bird in five years. I could hear Jaz's voice in my head, as clearly as if she was standing there next to me on the stairs.

"So how about it?" Dad was saying. "Are you going to come and visit?"

As his voice came down the line I could imagine him standing there in his Surrey mansion, pint mug in hand, wife and kiddies waiting in the background. The picture in my mind was so clear I could even see the old jumper he used to wear when chilling out at home on a Saturday. The only thing I couldn't picture, try as I might, was his face. I'd completely forgotten what he looked like. Funny, that.

"Maybe," I said, neutrally.

"And how about Molly? Alice said she was refusing to see me, but I'm sure you could persuade her."

"Possibly," I said, thinking as I said it, *no way*.

"I expect you're wondering why I wrote, like, out of the blue," he said, suddenly.

"It had crossed my mind," I confessed.

"The truth is, I don't really know. Perhaps it's my age – I was forty last year, you know."

I wondered if I ought to congratulate him. "Were you?" I said instead.

"Maybe it's a mid-life crisis or something." He gave another little laugh. "I just felt I should be putting my life in order. That kind of thing. You and Molly – I've always felt bad about you. Alice and I just couldn't rub along together, but you and Moll, you're flesh and blood."

"Yes."

"So, will you come? I'll send the train fare. Tell you what, I'll do better than that. I'll send the tickets. For both of you. First class. What d'you say?"

Rupert and Michael thundered past me, on

their way upstairs. I moved to one side to let them pass.

"Perhaps in the holidays – the Easter holidays, yeah?" I said. "I'll let you know. Give me your number, and I'll ring and let you know."

"Promise?"

"I promise," I said, solemnly.

"That's my girl."

"Dad?" It was no good; I had to ask him.

"What is it?"

"You know that time, just before we left, when you hit me?"

"*Hit* you?" His voice rose. "No, Mattie. I'd never have hit you. You must be mistaken. Your mother, yes. I put up my hand to that. I'm not proud of it, but I admit it. But never you or Molly. It must be something your mother's made up, feeding you a line over the years to turn you against me." He laughed again, a laugh of disbelief. "I'd never have hit you. Not my girl. Anyway, what were you going to ask me?"

"It doesn't matter now."

He gave me his address in Surrey and his telephone number, and after a few more exhortations to go and visit, he rang off. I sat there on the stairs, looking at the receiver in my hand. It felt strange that only seconds before I'd been speaking down it to my father;

it seemed almost magical, like some kind of modern day miracle, bringing my father back from the dead; or at any rate as good as dead for all the part he'd played in our lives since we'd been here in Devon.

I was just trying to work out how I was feeling about it all when a blood-curdling scream rang out from upstairs, making me jump in fright.

"COLIN!"

My master-stroke, my absolute *pièce de résistance*, was the old cuddly toy of Molly's I'd borrowed to add to the tableau. I'd opened the door of the rat's cage, laid it on its side and pulled some bedding out, to make it look as if there'd been a struggle. Then I'd put the toy (run underneath the bathroom tap beforehand) on the floor a little distance from the cage, with a length of crimson ribbon left over from Molly's pigtail-wearing days carefully arranged partly on top of it, partly across the carpet.

From only a few paces away, it looked remarkably like a bedraggled brown rat that had met a particularly nasty fate at the hands (or rather paws) of a much larger animal.

"Oh dear," I drawled, leaning against the door jamb and enjoying the little drama I'd created. "It looks like Colin's been disembowelled by next-door's cat. You really should keep your bedroom window closed."

Next to me, Rupert stood with his hands half covering his face, peeping out from between his fingers like a toddler watching something scary on telly, and sobbing fit to bust. It was magic – I couldn't have asked for more. *Vengeance is mine, saith the Bitch-Queen.*

I stood there for a few moments more, eking it out. Then I stepped forwards, picked up the teddy, ribbon and all, and lobbed it at Rupert.

"It's a fake, you pillock."

Rupert gave a little gasp and stepped back in horror, not daring to touch it or even look at it, but Michael bent down to inspect it.

"She's right," he declared, picking it up and brandishing it under Rupert's snotty nose. "It's a toy – look!"

I shook my head and tutted patronizingly, mimicking Rupert's usual smug attitude.

"All I can say is you must be loopy, Rupey, to fall for something as obvious as that."

Rupert's response took me utterly unawares. He let out an unearthly eldritch howl and flung himself at me in a kind of hysterical rugby tackle, knocking me to the floor and winding me as he landed on top of me.

"You bloody sodding *cow!*"

222

His face was millimetres from mine, his spittle-flecked lips drawn back from his teeth in a snarl. He was almost incoherent with rage, and so close to me I could feel his breath on my cheek.

"I'll kill you – I'll bloody *kill* you!"

He was surprisingly heavy; I couldn't move, couldn't dislodge him, couldn't ward him off. I felt his hands scrabbling at my throat. I turned my face away and closed my eyes, and for one terrible moment I truly believed he was going to kill me. Then I heard voices, Mum's and Geoffrey's and Molly's voices, all exclaiming and talking at once, and Rupert was pulled off me and hands were offered to help me to my feet. I ignored them and got up by myself, with as much dignity as I could muster.

I had to tell them where the real Colin was hidden, of course. Once they'd ascertained that Rupert hadn't just thrown a mental and attacked me out of the blue. They even seemed to think he'd been justified; this from Mum, who in her youth regularly used to attend peace rallies and anti-war demos.

"I thought you were against violence," I muttered, mutinously.

"So I am. But I can understand Rupert's reaction, even if I don't condone it. I'm ashamed of you, Mattie. It was a dreadful, cruel thing to do — you know how much he loves that rat. I can't imagine what possessed you to play such a mean trick on the poor child."

Useless to tell them about Ty'n Grhyn, of course: how could I spill the beans about that without them finding out the true nature of my relationship with Sam? Even when Colin was liberated from his hiding place and borne triumphantly by Rupert back upstairs to his cage, even when they could see for themselves how well I'd looked after him — what kind of terrorist buys their victims honey-coated rat treats, for Christ's sake? — even then, they still didn't forgive me. I could see the accusation in their eyes. Matilda Fry, the girl who torments poor motherless boys. God. It was enough to make me want to puke.

Even Molly turned against me. I suspected it was only because the rat had been involved: she always gets sentimental about animals.

"It was well mean," she told me. "I'm glad I didn't know you were planning it. I'd have told you not to do it."

I was speechless with the injustice of it, for all of ten seconds.

"I like that!" I spluttered indignantly. "Just who was it who started all the name-calling in the first place, pray? Where did Tin Grin come from originally — and Metal Mouth, and Track

Teeth, and all the other friendly little things you've been encouraging the whole lower school to call him?"

She had the grace to go red, at least. "Yeah, well," she muttered. "That's different."

"Only because that was you, and this is me!"

"Whatever. Anyway, I'm not going to tease him or call him names any more."

"Big deal."

"No, I mean it. I feel sorry for him. You didn't see the look on his face."

"Of course I didn't — he was half-strangling me at the time."

"I mean it, Mat." Her face was serious, and I could tell that she did indeed mean it. "We've been horrible to him for long enough. I think he's taken enough stick. Anyway," she went on, not quite meeting my eyes, "he's not so bad once you get used to him. I've been hanging out with him and Michael a bit just lately. We were all crabbing down at the cove earlier, and he was being really nice. And he didn't have to be, did he? Not when you consider how mean you and me have been to him."

It was clear she felt guilty. I didn't, though. I thought Rupert deserved everything coming to him. If Molly wanted to betray me and start consorting with the enemy, then fine. But she needn't think I was going to join in. No way.

It all blew over, of course, the Colin incident.
After a day or two everybody had forgotten all
about it. All except me. Phase One of my plan
– get even with Rupert – was over, even if it
hadn't gone quite as I'd intended. Now it was
time to put Phase Two into action – destroying
the evidence.

The very next time Rupert went out, I crept
into his room with the intention of expunging
the Hero Warrior from the face of the earth.
Or at least, deleting all the documents I could
find that featured him.

The peace and quiet of Rupert's room was
broken only by a rhythmic clattering sound. It
was Colin, running pointlessly round his wheel
with a rapt expression on his face.

"Hello mate." I bent down to greet him.
"Enjoy your little holiday, did you?"

It was strange how I could look at him with-
out shuddering now I'd destroyed his *alter ego*.
If only the same might be said of Rupert and
Ty'n Gryhn.

I sat down at the computer and moved the
mouse, clicking on the familiar document. *Fry*.
A blank screen came up. Funny… I pressed the
mouse again. Still nothing. I went back to the
desktop and opened everything that looked
vaguely likely. I discovered various homework

assignments, pompous complaining letters to the local paper, even another fantasy story in which the storyline was even weaker and the spelling and punctuation even worse (and featuring a hero called Roo P't but no Harridans or Bitch-Queens — obviously an earlier opus) — but no Ty'n Grhyn. He'd quite clearly wiped the whole lot himself.

I was just about to give up and leave Colin to exercise in peace when my eye was caught by another document called, innocuously, DAY#TO.DAY. *I wonder*, I thought. *I just wonder*. So I opened it, and that's how I discovered Rupert's diary.

chapter sixteen

Entry 306 – Star Date 7.45.2347.
When Dad came to bring me home for
halfterm today he had some pretty
worying news, he told me there was
someone he wanted me to meet in the
holidays. Well I knew at once he
meant A Woman. And it turns out its
even worse than that, its A Woman
With Children. I know I should
really be feeling glad for him etc
etc but the problem is I cant. I
keep thinking of mum, has he forgoten about her already? I won t
ever be able to. Dad says I'm
worying about nothing that just
becaus he wants us to meet hes not
planing to move in or anything. But
I'm not so sure. I've just got a
horid feeling about it all.

Entry 307 – Star Date 33.63.21094.
Met them today. They are not to bad
really. They are Mrs Fry and her

daughters Molly and Matilda. I felt dead strange when dad told me her name but she is known as Mattie, not Tilda like mum so that's all right. I think I was worying about nothing like dad said. Mrs Fry is OK (she was quite kind to me) but shes a bit of a weredo. No way is dad going to get marryed to someone like her.

Entry 308 — Star Date 1.58.346. Well it seems I was wrong. Dad has just told me he has asked mrs Fry to marry him and she has said yes. How can he? He has only just met her. How can I ever trust him again? He told me only a couple of days ago that he wasn't planing to move in, how can he do this, not to me but to mum. He must have completely forgoten about her. Or perhaps he never loved her in the first place. I will never forget her never never never. Mrs Fry might think she can take her place but she never will I wont let her.

Entry 309 — Star Date 62.8.3638. Had a long chat with dad today and feel a bit better. He told me he has known Mrs F for almost a year and she makes him happy. I cant really argue with that, after all he wasnt very happy the last year or so with mum even though that wasnt her fault. Anyway I shall be at school a lot of the time so perhaps it wont effect me much. Its nice seeing dad smiling and laughing again.

Entry 310 - Star Date 0.4257.28
Back at school now. I hate doing this in the IT room, I always think Fletcher is going to be looking over my sholder and telling all the others that I write a pansy diary. They are bound to say its a pansy diary. Just becase I dont like football they think they have a right to say what they like about me. I cant wait to leave at the end of term and go somewhere where theres life outside sport.

Entry 311 - Star Date 78.26352.8.
Mrs F sent me a postcard today, its of Brandy Bay where her cottage is.

Kind of her. V. pretty place, its nice to think of me and dad living there. Better than dad's flat at the uni at any rate. I supose as long as d. and me are together it doesnt matter much where it is.

Entry 312 — Star Date 9.5.2654556. Letter from dad today. Bad news. He says I will be going to school near brandy Bay after he & Mrs F are maried. A day boy. I dont mind that as such but I know I am likely to be picked on for having gone to bording school. I supose I will be picked on wherever I go because I look funny (specs, braces etc) but I know people at state schools really hate kids who have been to bording school. Marwells brother had to go to one because his parents didnt have the dosh to send him here and he wasnt clever enough for a scolarship and they held his head down the bog and flushed it every day he was there and they had to take him away eventully. Marwell says he nearly had a Nervos Breakdown. Dad says I'm worying about nothing but its all right for him, hes not the one who has to put up with being bullied. He doesnt know what its like.

Entry 313 — Star Date 92.7.24.
Dad came to see me today. Bart rang him up and said he was woried about me. Had a long chat, he told me he was bulied at school to so he does understand my feelings. He said we'll give St Marks (the school near B.bay) a go and see what its like and I can always leave and go somewhere else if its crap (but he didnt say crap of course HA HA.) I supose it will be easier because I will be able to go on the school bus with Matilda and Molly and I will at least know somebody there, if I went to public school I probly wouldnt know anybody. Dad told me to have a chat with Mr Simpson if I have any other worrys. Feel a bit better now.

Entry 314 — Star Date 924.83.5
The wedding is going to be in August. Decided am not going to

write any more of this while still at school, fed up with avoiding Fletcher, so thats it until the hols.

Entry 315.
Fed up with writing Star Date, totaly pointless. I dont know why I started it. Its dead childish. So its just the entry number from now on. First day of summer hols today and nothing much happened apart from new spot on nose. Fed up.

Entry 316.
Round at Frys today with dad. He and Mrs F talking about wedding the whole time, nothing for me to do. Boring.

Entry 317.
Getting a bit woried again about this wedding, well not so much the wedding as afterwards. Dont think Matilda and Molly like me very much. They havent said anything but its the way they look at me especialy Ma. (Mo. not quite so bad.) Ma. looks at me in just the

same way the sport fanaticks at
school, like just because I'm not
the same as them I come from
another planet or something. Dad
says I am imaginning things and
worying about nothing again.

Entry 318.
Guess what, I have been invited to
a party!!! Ma.s freind Jasmilla is
having a birthday party and I am
going to. Feel quite exited. Just
as long as I dont have to dance,
I'm useless at dancing.

Entry 319.
Round at Frys again today. I'm
definately not imaginning things.
Ma. keeps talking to me in this
funny voice, dead posh and with a
kind of lisp. I think shes trying
to imatate me but it doesnt sound
a bit like me. Shes the sort of
girl who thinks shes great, quite
pretty in a tomboy kind of way
(always wears trousers) but to full
of herself. Confidant. Mrs F showed
me a catalog with all these trendy
clothes in, she said I'd want

something new to wear to the party.
Dad says she was only trying to be
helpfull and I supose it was kind
of her but it made me wish mum was
around instead to help me chose. I
was upset this evening and dad was
kind and said he misses mum to. But
the thing he doesnt really understand is that hes getting a new
wife but I can never have a new
mother.

Entry 320.
Party. Quite good really. Met someone called Micheal, hes a top bloke
and will be in my year at St Marks
so thats alright. Grub was pretty
decent to. And Ma.s freind Jasmilla
is dead pretty. I couldnt help
watching her all evening shes got
beatiful long black hair (it
reminded me a bit of mums before it
all fell out during the treatment.)
But I know a pretty girl like her
would never ever look at someone as
ugly as me. Perhaps when I'm older
and my spots and braces have gone
I can get contact lenses and that
will make me look a bit more

235

normal. Micheal and I agree that girls dont know what its like being a boy, all they have to do is sit around waiting to be asked out or to dance or whatever while we boys always have to do the asking. Its suposed to be different now but it isnt really, I'd love a girl to ask me out but I know they never will. Girls dont want to know boys like me.

Anyway it was a good party. Ma. got off with some bloke who looks like tarzan (masive mussles) and it was quite funny because her trousers got riped and everyone could see her nickers. She got in a bate when I told her but I was only doing her a favor wasnt I (ha ha).

Entry 321.
At Frys again. Ma. and Mo. showed me Brandy bay and dad made me go swiming, I wish he hadnt he knows I hate it specialy in the sea. I asked him afterwards why he'd made me and he said he thought it was important I was seen to be making an efort and joining in. I dont

know why I should be the only one
making an efort. I cant see Ma.
making much of an efort, all she
does is talk at me in that stupid
voice all the time. I think shes a
bit of a cow and am beginning to
wonder what living in the same
house will be like. (Mo. isnt so
bad I must say.)
Tarzan (from the party) turned up
and he and Ma. were flirting all
over the beech. Its obvios they
fancy each other. Why cant I look
like him and be atractive to girls?
(not that I want Ma. to fancy me,
no chance. Jasmilla would be nice
though.)

Entry 322.
Started a new story. Havent done
anything on Roo P't for yonks (got
bord with it) but am quite into
this one now. Featuring a new hero
called Ty'n Grhyn (thats what Mo.
& Ma. call me, they dont think Ive
heard them but I have.) Basicaly he
gets to conker the Kingdom of Fry
(geddit?) and win the hand of the
fair maiden J'Asmil Aa and then he

goes on to change his name to Roo
P't and basicaly rule the world.
Spent all day today writing it, I'm
dead pleased with it. Going to ask
dad if Micheal can come round for
tea and then he can maybe read it
and make sugestions, I know hes
into fantasy stories (dungons &
dragons etc) like me.
This time next week dad & Mrs F
will be maried. Makes me feel funny
to think about it so not going to.

Entry 323. Entry 1 of New Life.
Havent written this for yonks. Will
try to rember things that hapened
but its hard, in fact I dont want
to rember a lot of it.
Well dad and mrs F are now marryed
and I am writing this in my bedroom
in the cottage at B. Bay (it used
to be Mo.s bedroom but now its
mine. Boy did that cause problems.
But thats one of the things I dont
want to remeber.)
The wedding itself was all right I
suppose if you like that kind of
thing. Fletcher would say it was
pansy. Dad loked so happy and it

238

made me feel wierd, part of me was glad (really really glad) that he was happy but the other biggest part was thinking about mum. I know she died nearly 2 years ago now but I couldn't help thinking about her all through that wedding day, it felt like she was truly being buryed at last. Everyone had forgoten about her apart from me and she was being shoved into the past while all everyone could talk about was the future.

Then we all went away on holiday together, it was suposed to be a honey moon but thats ridiclous, honey moons are only for the bride and bride groom and we were all there I mean how can that be called a honey moon? Stupid.

It was in the Lake District. Bad move. Theres nothing to do there but go walking and it rained all the time. I mean ALL THE TIME. I tryed sugesting we stayed in a few times but nobody listened to me, they all wanted to go out on the stupid crappy hills the whole time. I have never been so wet in my intire life. Then to cap it all Mo. & Ma. began teasing me the whole time, calling me names etc etc, I tryed not to take any notice but it was hard. Specialy when they called me loopy roopy, I know it was stupid but that upset me most of all because it made me think of mum. Anyway dad took me back to the carpark and we had a long chat, he told me to try and bear up and that Ma. was finding it dificult to and that the only way she could show it was by torementing me. Not sure I agree with that but anyway I said I'd try and then the so called honey moon was over Thank God and then we came back here and moved in. Wasnt sorry to leave that flat behind but cant help wondering what life here will be like insted. Phew. Long entry. V. tired now.

Entry 324/2 of New Life.
Feel better today. Mrs F trying to be kind but Ma. still being a cow. I am calling her the Harridan Bitch-Queen in my story, Micheal has been round and we have done some work on

it together. It will be nice to have a freind at the new school (St Marks) allthough dad now tells me I wont be in his year after all but in year 10 because the school aparently think I am to clever to be in year 9. That again. That word clever folowed me around Tamley Hall until I was sick of it. I wish I wasnt clever and looked normal insted, more people might like me then.

Entry 325/3 of N. L.
Not much hapened today except tarzan (mussel man from Jasmilla's party) came round to see Ma. this evening which was quite funny. Decided to use my tracking skills and folowed them (secretely) onto the beach and into the cave where they had a massive SNOG!!! Nearly died laughing, so did Micheal when told him later on phone. Never been so close to real life snogging couple before, quite intresting in slurpy kind of way.

Entry 4 of N. L.
Missing mum today. I start at st

marks tomorow and really wish she
was here to tell me everything will
be ok, dad trys but its not the
same and mrs f cant posibly know
how i feel because shes not my
mother so she neednt even bother
trying and I wish everyone would
justtttttttttttttttttt can't write
any more tonight sorry

Entry 5 of N. L.
St Marks not to bad I supose. Had
lunch with Micheal & he intraduced
me to some of his mates who seem ok.
Ma. hanging round with tarzan (real
name Sam). Micheal told me he (Sam
not Micheal) was Doing It with some
other girl in the hols (only
Micheal didnt say doing it he said
shagging.) Wonder if Ma. knows.

Entry 6 of N. L.
School. OK but nothing specal. Mo.
calling me names again wich I hate
but will rise above it.

Entry 7.
Mo. still calling me names & others
now joining in.

Entry 8.
Name calling still going on. I thought Mo. wasnt to bad, I've changed my mind now. St Marks even worse than Tamley Hall.

Entry 9.
Hate St marks. Hate Mo. & Ma. Hate everyone. Wish mum was here. Why did she have to die, its not fair.

Entry 10.
Feel better today. Went to Micheals after school, his house is great and his mum is cool. Wish I could go and live there. Did more work together on story (took disk), its really going well now.

Entry 11.
Major blow up at home today. Dont know what it was about exactly but involved dad and mrs F and Ma. — heard her shouting — "hes not my father" and felt a bit sorry for her becuase I know how that feels (only not with father of course.) Went & knocked on her door to see if she was ok but she was dead

huffy with me & made me wish I
hadnt bothered. Cow.

Entry 12.
More name calling at school, its
worse than ever. Asked dad if I
could move schools after christmas
but he says no. He says I havent
given it a fare crack of the whip.
Its all right for him he doesnt
have to put up with it.

Entry 13.
Went to see headmaster today who
asked me how I'd feel about moving
up a year for maths. Also said dad
had mentoned I was being picked on
and wondered what might help. Dont
know. Dont see how moving me up for
maths will help, it will probly
just give them more amumition to
fire at me.

Entry 13.
In new maths class today and guess
what? its Ma.s class. Just my luck.
Then to make matters worse the
teacher went and told everyone I
was her stepbrother and everyone

244

turned and starred. Why do I have to be clever. Why cant I just be the same as everyone else and look ordnary. Its not fair.

Entry 14.
New zits on chin & forhead today. They will be calling me pizza face soon as well as all the other things, Micheals brother David says he used to be called that. Still he has no spots now so maybe theres hope for me. Round at Micheals after school and saw Jasmilla in garden, keep forgeting she lives next door. She smiled at me and said hello. Shes so pretty and you can tell shes a really nice person to (wonder why shes so freindly with Ma.) so not a bad day despite new erruptions on face. Hols start tomorow.

Entry 15.
Havent written this for yonks because of christmas. It was ok but I always miss mum more than ever at christmas.

Entry 16.
More problems at home with Ma. Shes
now saying she wants to see her
father again. Its up to her I
supose but you can tell Mrs F isnt
to happy with the idea.

Entry 17.
Off school today with flu. Nobody
else home & got really bored. Went
into Mo. & Ma.s room while they
were at school and read Ma.s diary.
What a hoot. Full of love stuff
about Sam. Never did tell her about
him shagging that other girl. Looks
from her diary like shes thinking
of doing it with him to. Wonder
what mrs F would say (not that I'd
tell her I'm not like that.) Took
my mind off flu anyway ha ha.

Entry 18.
Ma. being really horible to me even
though I'm not well. I hate her.
Want my mum to make me feel better.

Entry 19.
Back at school just in time for
exams. Lucky me. Name calling not

quite as bad, Micheal says theyve
probly forgotten all about it.
Ignore last entry, its pathetick.

Entry 20.
No such luck. Its started again.

Entry 21.
Exam results. I think mixed is the
word. Good for maths, IT, sciences,
ok hist, geog, awful english &
french. Know my spellings useless
but didnt think I was that bad at
english. Decided will get rid of
the story (Ty'n Grhyn) as its crap,
its no use pretending its good
becuase it isnt. Hope dad isnt to
angry about exam results.

Entry 22.
Dad wasnt angry at all. Actualy I
dont really mind getting some bad
results, it makes me feel more
normal.

Entry 23.
Nearly got caught listning outside
Ma.s door today. Not that you need
to be standing right by the door to

247

know whats going on inside. Dad &
Mrs F must be thick if they really
beleive she & Sam are revising, for
a start the exams are over.

Entry 24.
That cow Matilda stole Colin and
pretended hed been killed by a cat.
I can cope with her being horible
to me but I dont know why she had
to involve colin, hes just a poor
dumb creture. She called me loopy
roopy again and this time I was so
angry I hit her. i thought of my
mother slowly dying of that brain
tumor and first not knowing dad and
me and then going totaly mad and I
thought I bet Matilda Fry has never
seen anybody really loopy, shes
lucky and if she calls me loopy
again I shall hit her and then I
did. I didnt think I was going to
stop. She made me do that to her
and Ive never hit anyone before in
my intire life, not even when
Fletcher spread that lie around
that I am gay (wich I'm not, I
fancy Jasmilla so I cant be can I.)
I HATE Matilda SO MUCH I dont know

why she is being such a BITCH to me
when I've never done anything to
her exept come and live in her
house and I didnt ask to do that
did I.

Entry 25.
Was so angry last night forgot to
say the worst bit. Dad is going to
america in the easter hols, hes
going for 3 weeks and I have to
stay here. I asked to go with him
and I begged him to let me go &
stay with gran like I used to when
he was at the old universty but he
says I cant. He says the americans
wont pay for me to go with him and
he cant aford to pay for me and
that gran is to old now for me to
stay for 3 weeks. I begged and
begged and I even cried although I
didnt mean to. I cant bear the
thought of being here without him
for 3 weeks I just cant bear it.

Entry 26.
Dad says I have to. He said chin up
old man its not that bad. How does
he know how bad it is. I HATE THE

FRYS ALL OF THEM I WISH THEY WERE
ALL DEAD INSTED OF MY MUM WHO NEVER
HURT ANYONE IN HER LIFE AND I WISH
THEY

chapter seventeen

That was it. There was no more.

Rupert's account of the past – what? – nearly twelve months had taken me only minutes to read, and I sat now motionless, staring at the screen with my hand still on the mouse.

When I'd started to read what he'd written I'd had a good snigger about his hopeless spelling, the utter lack of sophistication in his writing; I felt a kind of scornful amusement, almost a pleasure, that his cleverness obviously didn't extent to these things: good at Maths he may be, but English clearly wasn't one of his better subjects. As I read, I carefully stored away certain little details to share and laugh about later.

But as I read on the amusement dropped away, and in its place came other less comfortable feelings. I'd had pangs of remorse before at my treatment of him, but nothing like I was feeling now. I felt guilty as hell. What can I say? Guilty, ashamed, remorseful: yeah, all that and more. I realized that, in all the time since the Hortons had entered our lives, I had never once stopped to consider how Rupert might have felt: about us, and the fact of our sudden, unasked-for presence in his life; about his appearance, or the pains and insecurities of adolescence. I simply hadn't given it a thought, that he might not have wanted to become a part of Molly's and my life any more than we wanted him there, nor that he might be unhappy and self-conscious about the way he looked, his glasses and his braces and his deeply un-hip appearance.

Nor, it seemed to me more importantly, had I given a moment's thought to his feelings about losing his mother: neither had I bothered to wonder how she had died. A relatively young woman — about my mother's age, most likely — dead the past two years, and it hadn't occurred to me why. I had just accepted it. The truth, I suppose, the rather nasty unpalatable truth, was simply that I hadn't been interested.

But I was interested now all right, although perhaps interested isn't quite the right word. Appalled, maybe. Appalled to discover that the cause of her death had been a brain tumour, according to Rupert's unemphatic, almost throw-away account. A brain tumour, with all the attendant loss of dignity and bodily functions and faculties and other assorted horrors for family and friends to come to terms with and observe and deal with.

Just what had Rupert had to deal with? Just how much of his mother's slow and painful decline had he had to witness? I could scarcely bear to think about it. And why had nobody told me about it? I would never have called him Loopy Rupey if I had known, never; I wasn't that cruel.

Or was I? The unpleasant realization dawned on me that I probably was. Surely common sense should have told me, right from the start, that a lad of Rupert's age – of *any* age – would be missing his so recently dead mother. I had made no allowances for that whatsoever, instead I'd latched on to the way he looked and talked and set out to make life miserable for him in the most hurtful and childish ways imaginable.

And then it occurred to me that, even if Rupert's diary had contained no revelations or surprises and had continued to provide me with amusement to its end, I had nobody to share the joke with. Jaz and I were barely speaking since she'd told me of the rumour circulating about me and Sam and I'd refused to believe what she was saying. Sam himself wouldn't have been interested in anything Rupert had done, his sole mission in life so far as I was concerned apparently being to get me into bed. Molly, accused by me of betrayal and consorting with the enemy, was virtually ignoring me. Even my relationship with Mum was at an all-time low. We'd always been so close and got on so well, but now it had reached the stage where we couldn't even speak to each other without me snarling and her trying to be ever-so-understanding, which simply had the effect of winding me up even tighter.

What a bitch I must seem, I thought viciously. *A miserable, insensitive, spiteful bitch, and no friends to boot*. The double whammy. I hadn't enjoyed reading about Rupert's opinion of me, but what I had discovered about myself I liked a whole lot less.

In all honesty, my new-found self-knowledge didn't have much of a bearing on my relationship with Rupert. I mean, we didn't fall on each other's necks and swear undying friendship, or anything puke-making like that. The point was, I didn't actually like him any more than I had previously, I just felt sorry for him. But it was a compassionate feeling sorry rather than a pitying one, if that makes sense. It was enough to make me stop taking the mick and taunting him at every conceivable opportunity. He didn't seem to notice, although perhaps it was best that he didn't. It might have looked a bit suss, otherwise. How could I explain my change of heart without confessing to having read his diary?

One effect it did have was to make me examine my newly discovered relationship with my father. My motivation, as Mum had put it. In the cold light of day, I couldn't imagine what had made me decide to write back to him. What was he to me now? Nothing, was the stark answer; and he had been nothing to me for years. We hadn't heard from him since we left, as I've already said, but the fact was I had barely given him a thought in all those years, apart from recently. I hadn't been sitting moonily around, missing him and yearning to see him again. If I'd thought of him at all it was in the most damning of terms. We were well shot of him, is what I'd thought, and no matter how much I considered it now I couldn't in all honesty summon up any evidence to the contrary.

The one memory of him that had stuck in my mind all those years, of him slamming his fist into my ten-year-old face in a terrible fit of rage and temper, he couldn't even remember. I had been so sure of his regret for that incident, so convinced that he would ever since have been living with the dreadful memory of having punched his small daughter; but all the time he had just forgotten about it.

I can't even begin to explain how that made me feel, except that it told me I'd made a big mistake in contacting him. An opinion which, as it turned out, he clearly shared.

On the morning of my birthday, a Saturday, I came downstairs to find the usual crop of cards sitting by my plate.

Mum said, "Happy birthday, darling", and kissed me. Molly was upstairs somewhere: Geoffrey had gone to the university to finalize arrangements for his trip to the States in a week or so. Rupert had had a sleepover at Michael's. It didn't feel like my birthday, and I wasn't anyway in the mood for celebrations.

"Thanks." I sat down and took a piece of toast.

"Aren't you going to open your cards?"

"Later." I pushed them to one side, and began spreading the toast with butter.

"Mattie." Mum put her hand over mine. "What's wrong?"

What's wrong? Only my whole life. "Nothing."

"But it's your birthday. You've always loved birthdays."

"Yeah. Well, I'm sixteen now, aren't I? Grown up, more or less. Maybe it's about time I stopped loving them and started dreading them."

"Sweetheart, it's not like you to be so

256

cynical." Mum took her hand off mine, picked up the top card from the pile and held it out to me. "This is from me."

"You and Geoffrey. Thanks."

"No, just me. The card from Geoffrey and me is the next one." She extended her arm. "Do open it, darling."

I put my knife down and took the envelope, inserting my finger under the flap and ripping open the thin paper. Inside was a cheque for a hundred pounds.

"Mum, it's——" I was speechless. Ridiculous tears sprang to my eyes. "It's really generous of you. Thanks so much. I don't know what to say…"

"I thought money was the best thing." She looked pleased, taking pleasure from my pleasure.

"It's such a lot. Can you afford it?"

A hundred pounds was two weeks' food shopping, shoes for Mum and Molly and me, enough paint to redecorate the entire cottage, a new toilet cistern to replace the one that had been cracked and repaired and re-repaired since time immemorial. There was never enough money to go around, never had been, and she had just given me a hundred pounds.

"Of course I can. I've been saving up."

We both stood up, at the same time, and gave

257

each other a hug; clumsily at first, but then with real and growing warmth and love.

"Happy birthday," she whispered, into my hair, and I was suddenly and piercingly reminded of birthdays past, of times we'd hugged when I'd only come up to her breast-bone, when I'd been her little girl and she my strong capable mum with the power to right all the wrongs in my puny little life.

How times had changed. The tears pricked behind my eyelids again, and one escaped and tracked its way down my nose and under my cheek to the corner of my mouth; but it was a tear of self-pity, and I wiped it away crossly.

"Right," I said, and sat down again. "Let's have a look at these other cards."

Mum talked to me while I was opening them, about what I could spend the money on, and the birthday meal she was going to cook for me that night, suggesting I ring Jaz and Sam and invited them too.

"If they're free," she said. "Perhaps I should have mentioned it before."

"Yeah, right," I said, with a grin. "Mum's famous organizational skills strike again."

I didn't tell her Jaz was almost certain to be doing something else of a Saturday night. She hadn't shown much inclination of late to spend time with me. And as for Sam, I couldn't honestly say I had a great deal of inclination to spend time with him at the moment. Our relationship seemed to be characterized by periods of red-hot lust (on both sides), followed by ones of ice-cool apathy (also on both sides). I was definitely going through one of the latter phases at the moment, and wasn't quite sure why. Nothing Sam had done, or not done – just too much else going on in my life, I suppose.

I'd reached the last envelope in the pile. The handwriting on the front was familiar: I looked at it idly for a moment or two, turning it over in my hands, before slitting it open and drawing out the contents.

It was from my father: a birthday card and, inside, a letter stating in the baldest of terms that he had decided after all not to continue the contact he'd resumed with me.

Rosie was very upset at the idea, the letter read, *she says the past is best left in the past, so I think it's best that you don't come to visit after all. I hope you don't think too badly of me, and would like to take the opportunity to wish you a happy birthday and all the best for the future.*

"What is it?" Mum was asking. "What's the matter? Who's it from?"

"Dad," I said, shortly, and tossed it across the table at her.

She read it in a second. When she looked up at me, her face was dark with an emotion I didn't recognize.

"Mattie," she said, and then we were up on our feet and hugging each other again.

"He's a bastard," she said, her voice filled with uncharacteristic vehemence. "I'm so sorry. You didn't deserve that, to be picked up and then put down again with such unthinking, such *casual*..." Her voice trailed off, angrily.

"I don't care," I said fiercely, over and over. "I don't care, I don't care."

But the truth was I did care, very much. Despite having already made up my mind not to go and see him, having him make the unilateral decision like that hurt like hell. I wanted to be the one to decide, to tell him I'd changed my mind. I wanted the satisfaction of telling him I'd misjudged him when I'd thought he regretted the past, that any man who hit his ten-year-old daughter and then forgot about it was the lowest of the low. But now he'd deprived me of that, just as in the past he'd deprived Mum and Molly and me of a normal family life. *Thanks, Dad. Thanks a million. And I hope you have a nice life, too.*

Back at school, after the weekend, Jaz gave me a present.

"Happy birthday, she said. "Sorry it's late. We were away over the weekend."

Her eyes didn't quite meet mine.

It was a velvet scarf, hand-painted in vivid turquoises and violets, and quite beautiful.

"It's lovely," I said, truthfully, and taken aback.

She put an arm round my shoulders and gave me a hug. Jaz and me don't have that kind of girly, touchy-feely friendship, so I was taken aback by that, too.

"I've missed you," she said. "Can we please start talking again? I always swore I'd never let a lad come between me and my mates."

To my embarrassment I felt my eyes well up again. I seemed to be close to tears a lot of the time these days. What was the matter with me?

I looked down at the scarf, to buy time.

"Sure," I said, at last. "I've missed you too."

"And for the record," she said, softly, "it wasn't me who spread that rumour."

"Right."

"And something else, too. Sam and Vanessa have split up."

I looked at her, suspiciously, a tiny pang of some curious unidentifiable emotion passing through me.

"How do you know all these things? How come you get to hear them and I don't?"

I suddenly realized what the feeling was. *Triumph*. He was mine, after all. Vanessa was history.

"Connections," she said airily, and shrugged. "It's no big deal. Surjit's girlfriend told me – Naomi. She's big buddies with Vanessa. Vanessa's devastated, apparently: Sam told her he was bored with her and anyway he's got somebody else. Can you imagine! The mean sod!"

Jaz could call him what she liked, it didn't bother me. *He's got somebody else.* Yeah, me. I'd been right all along, and couldn't summon any pity for Vanessa. As far as I could see, she'd been trespassing on my turf from the beginning.

Sam gave me a birthday present, too. He came round that evening, unannounced, bearing a box of chocolate truffles and a big bunch of daffodils. I was touched: nobody had ever bought me flowers before. Not a lad, at any rate.

"Come on in," I said, holding the door open with one hand and the flowers in the other. God, he was truly beautiful. How could I have imagined I'd gone off him? It was all very well being indifferent to him when I wasn't seeing much of him, but all he had to do was stand in front of me and smile that smile, and that was it. I was done for. And boy, did he know it.

"Well, come on," I repeated, stepping back a pace. "Come and help me eat the chocs."

Sam said, "I can't," his mouth twisting with regret. "Gotta get back. But look, I'll see you at school, yeah? There's something I want to show you — a surprise."

I wanted to know what it was, of course, but he wouldn't tell, just climbed on to his bike with a grin and an elegant swing of his leg (how *do* lads manage that manoeuvre?) and rode off fast, up the killer hill.

I didn't have to wait long to find out. Sam's surprise was the place he'd told me about, the cosy place where we wouldn't get disturbed, where he was planning to seduce me. If seduce is the right way of putting it, which it probably isn't. After all, I'd given him all the signals which told him I was as keen as him. My only surprise was that he'd held off for as long as he had; he'd not mentioned it since the incident when I caught Rupert listening outside the bedroom door, and I certainly hadn't mentioned it. I'd rather hoped he'd forgotten about it, or given up trying. I was wrong on both counts.

We met after lunch, and went together to the school hall and the room behind the stage. It was a quite ordinary classroom, used for lessons during the day and as a changing room cum warming-up room for school productions or concerts. It was quite unremarkable, with the usual tables and chairs, the teacher's desk, and a cupboard at the back. The cupboard door was locked – Sam tried the handle and rattled it, noisily.

"What are we doing here?" I was fidgety, uneasy, aware that we shouldn't be in there and that the bell for afternoon registration would be going any minute.

"Hang about."

Sam fished in his pocket and produced a key, which he fitted into the lock of the cupboard. He turned the handle, and the door swung open.

"Open sesame!" He turned to me, grinning. "There you go. Our *boudoir*. What d'you reckon?"

He pronounced it boo-doyer, but I didn't bother correcting him. I stepped past him and looked into the cupboard which wasn't a cupboard at all, but a small windowless room leading off the first. It was full of piles of dusty old scenery from previous school productions, clothes rails packed with assorted costumes, and unravelling wicker hampers overflowing with what looked like velvet curtains. I hadn't known it existed.

I turned back to Sam. "How come you've got a key?"

"I was helping with the scenery and stuff when they did *Oliver* last term. Andy and me used to come in at weekends to paint the flats, and Simkins gave me a key. He never asked for it back afterwards: reckon he forgot I had it."

He flicked on the switch by the door, and the room was filled with light. Throwing back the lid of one of the hampers, he pulled out a length of the curtains and showed it to me, draping the faded velvet across his arms like a tailor showing off his wares.

"What d'you reckon?" he repeated.

"It's not really my colour," I muttered, under my breath.

He looked at me, sharply. "What?"

"Nothing."

"So, what d'you think? We could pull out all these old curtains and put them on the floor, make a kind of..."

"Bed," I said, helpfully.

"I was going to say nest, but yeah; bed, if you like."

He put the curtain down and put an arm round my waist, with a leer. He clearly liked.

"Not now, though," I said, hastily, dissembling. "The bell's going in a tick. They'll be using this room for lessons. It's too risky."

"I didn't mean now." He looked put out, pouting slightly, like a little kid who couldn't get his own way. "I just wondered what you thought. As a general concept."

"Fine."

What did I mean, fine? He was planning to relieve me of my virginity, and all I could say was "Fine"?

"After school some time then, yeah? We can sneak back when everyone's gone, and lock the door behind us. There'll be no chance of anyone disturbing us then."

So that's how I found myself, at the end of the week, tiptoeing back into the room with Sam. It was clear I'd put him off for long enough; this time, I simply hadn't been able to come up with a plausible reason for saying no. I was petrified, to be honest: not, curiously enough, at the prospect of what lay ahead, but of the possibility of being caught.

"Relax," Sam told me, closing the door carefully behind us. "It's Friday. All the staff push off early for the weekend. Even if anyone was around, nobody'll be coming in here. Why would they?"

He began taking the curtains from the hampers and strewing them around the floor, heaping them up a little to form a mound. It did look very comfortable. I found myself watching him in a detached kind of way, as if what he was doing bore no relevance to me whatsoever. It seemed very odd, unreal, to think we were both going to lie down on that soft velvet cushion and…

"Give us a hand, will you?" Sam shoved a curtain into my hands. "Just put it there, at the top."

I did as he bid me, thinking as I did so how similar it felt to the childish games of making house Molly and I used to play when we were kids. About a hundred years ago.

There was nothing remotely childish about the game we were playing now. Sam produced a torch from his pocket and snapped off the main light.

"More romantic," he pronounced.

Then we lay down together on the bed we had created. Sam began to kiss me. My heart was beating so fast it sounded like a steam-hammer: surely Sam could hear it too? He undid my school tie and blouse, kissing me at intervals, and then removed them. He sat up, briefly, and pulled his own shirt over his head, then lay down and embraced me again, skin against skin.

"This is it, baby," he murmured. "You're sixteen now. It's all legal. There's nothing to stop us."

Nothing to stop us. Through my mind went the little phrase Mum had trotted out, centuries ago, when telling me about the facts of life. I'd already known what she was telling me, had picked it all up long ago through the usual playground sources, but had been too embarrassed to tell her so.

One day you'll meet someone you really love, and you'll respect each other and want to have this sort of loving relationship.

Did Sam respect me? Did I respect him? I knew the answer to both those questions.

Nothing to stop us.

Then I thought, *What the hell. I've got to lose it some time. It may as well be with someone I really fancy. And as it's already all over school we've been doing it, what have I got to lose?*

Sam pushed my skirt up my thighs, and then pulled away from me for a second and thrust his hand in his trouser pocket.

"We'll need these," he said, gruffly. "I don't suppose you've got yourself fixed up."

I looked at what he was holding. It was a packet of condoms, the cellophane already ripped. He opened the packet, and I could see it wasn't full.

"Don't worry. I know what I'm doing. You'll be OK."

I know what I'm doing. The packet was already opened. He'd done this before. With another stupid, gullible fool who'd believed his lies about being in love. Or fools, plural.

I sat up, abruptly, grabbing my shirt and holding it across my chest in a rather belated attempt at modesty.

"What are you doing?"

"Forget it," I told him. "Just forget it, OK? I've got no intention of being just another notch on your bedpost."

His face was close to mine, illuminated oddly by the Hallowe'en light of the torch. I saw frustration flash behind his eyes and his mouth opened in angry protest, but I was spared his reply because at that precise moment the door opened and the room was suddenly flooded with harsh fluorescent light as the switch was snapped on.

chapter eighteen

What can I tell you about the aftermath? Only
that it was, without question, the most
scorchingly humiliating experience of my life. I
thought Simkins was going to have a heart
attack, catching us there *in flagrante delicto*, as
he put it later.

Much later. Like, Monday. We had the whole
weekend to think about what had happened, to
worry about what was going to happen, to go
over and over it in our minds and wonder what
in the name of God had possessed us to put
ourselves in such a ridiculously risky situation
in the first place.

That's what went through *my* mind, at any
rate, over and over, until I longed for Monday
morning to come and put me out of my misery.
I don't suppose Sam did much soul-searching.
He didn't look especially bothered, either
before the roasting or after it, as if he got caught
in cupboards with half-naked girls every day of
the week. Perhaps he did. How would I know?

"It's the kind of stunt this school's come to
expect of you," Simkins said to Sam.

Coming from anybody else, Sam would have taken it as a compliment. Not from Simkins, though.

"But you," he went on repressively, looking at me. There was such scorn in that look, such utter contempt. I felt that look burning into my soul for months afterwards. "What in the name of all that's holy came over you? What made you let this – this *boy*," (waving a contemptuous hand towards Sam), "degrade and debauch you in such a filthy way?"

And on, and on, until I wanted to just sink into the ground and disappear under a welter of shame and mortification.

"Well," Sam said to me, afterwards, pushing a hand through the front of the hair in that familiar way that used to make me go weak at the knees. Now, it just made me want to slap him. "That wasn't so bad, was it?"

"Wasn't it?" I turned on him, suddenly furious. "So what would you call bad, then?"

"He did say he wasn't going to take it any further. He's not going to tell the head. It could have been worse."

I couldn't think of a single way in which it could have been worse, and told him so.

"And I thought you'd locked the door," I added pathetically.

"Yeah, well, I forgot. In the heat of the

moment. Shame Simkins took the key away. I don't suppose…"

He eyed me, up and down, and the blood rose to my face in a hot angry tide.

"Don't even think about it. I never want to see you again, Sam Barker."

He shrugged. "No loss to me. Who wants to be seen with a slag like you? Anyway, I only went out with you in the first place because of a bet."

He walked off down the corridor, hands in pockets, whistling nonchalantly and leaving me standing there alone with my thoughts. They weren't very good company.

"Are you OK?"

I turned round: it was Andy Cooper.

"Oh yeah, just fab. Never better. Just—" and to my horror I burst into tears.

Andy manoeuvred me into a conveniently empty classroom, sat me down, and let me sob. After a bit, when I was getting a grip, he handed me a handkerchief.

"It is clean," he told me. "Have a good blow, you'll feel better."

He was wrong.

"Thanks. Look, I'd better be going."

I held the hanky out to him, but he shook his head.

"Keep it. Look, call me nosey, tell me to mind my own business, but was it Sam?"

"How did you guess." I looked down at the hanky and began twisting it between my fingers.

"I'm psychic." He glanced at me. "No I'm not. He told me what had happened, about you both getting caught by Simkins."

"He told you?" I was furious. "And you both had a good laugh about it, no doubt. I suppose you think I'm a slag, too."

"Is that what he called you?"

"Yeah. And he said he only went out with me for a bet. A bet with you, I suppose. And they say the age of chivalry is dead."

I went to push my chair back and get up, but Andy stopped me.

"Hang about. For a start, I don't think you're a slag."

"No? The rest of the school seems to."

"No. And for a second, he didn't go out with you for a bet."

"Oh yeah; and you'd know all about that!"

"That's right. He went out with you to prove a point."

"And the point is?"

"That he can get any girl he chooses. No matter what the competition."

I frowned. "Sorry, you've lost me."

"It's quite simple. I told him I liked you, so he had to ask you out."

"You told him——?"

"I liked you. Yeah."

"Oh." I couldn't think what else to say.

"And I still do."

"Even though I'm a slag?"

"Mattie…" He leant forward. "You're not. No one thinks that."

"They do. They think I've been sleeping with him. It's all round school." The tears came to my eyes again, and I dabbed at them with Andy's hanky.

"It's a five-minute wonder. They've forgotten about it already." He put out a hand and touched my shoulder. "Mattie, nobody believes it. They know you. And they know Sam. C'mon, honestly – who would you believe?"

Put like that, he did have a point.

"Are you sure?"

"Sure I'm sure."

"Why did you let Sam ask me out?"

He laughed shortly. "Like I had a choice. How could I stop him? What Sam wants, Sam gets."

"But you're still mates." This male bonding thing was a mystery to me. "I told him I never wanted to see him again."

"Don't blame you. He treats girls shockingly, I've always told him he'd get his comeuppance and now he has."

"Has he? How?"

"He's lost you, hasn't he?"

"Big deal." I grimaced.

"He did like you, you know. It wasn't just the physical. He always said you were too classy for him. He must be kicking himself, now."

"You don't have to be kind to me, you know, Andy."

"I'm not being kind."

"Yes you are. I know I'm not in the usual league of Sam's girlfriends."

"Don't be a nit." He spoke affectionately. "Look at you, you're..." He trailed off, suddenly shy, and cleared his throat. "You're beautiful."

And for an odd moment, even in my tear-stained, chastened and humiliated state, he really made me feel that I was.

chapter nineteen

So life was beginning to look up. Just a tad, but definitely up. Jaz and I were back to normal. Mum and I were rubbing along much better now thanks to my father showing himself in his true colours, which also had the effect of resolving that particular episode. Now it was over, I couldn't quite believe I'd seriously contemplated actually meeting up with him again. How could I have excused him all the years of pain followed by all the years of silence, ended by him purely on a whim? How could I have contemplated being a pawn in his pathetic mid-life crisis? There had been no word of apology or regret, yet I'd been prepared to forgive him everything just to — what? Show Mum and Geoffrey I still had a father, a *real* father? I had fiercely denied it at the time, but I couldn't deny that's exactly what it looked like.

And the whole Sam thing was over too, painfully but irrevocably, and I felt no regrets for that but only a deep sense of relief that I wouldn't have to fend him off any more. I'd thought I was in control of the situation, but I clearly hadn't been. Something else I'd learnt was that I definitely wasn't ready for a physical relationship with anyone, no matter how much I might fancy them.

I was even beginning to get used to having Rupert around: strange but true. Reading his diary had given me an insight into his feelings, an awareness of other people's pain rather than just my own.

I reflected how strange life was, that the most painful knocks are what we ultimately learn most from. I was beginning to feel I could relax a bit now, that so many different elements in my life had conspired to come together and give me a hard time, but now I was coming through. There was sunshine after the rain, light at the end of the tunnel, and other assorted clichés. That's what I thought, anyway.

Until I got home from school, the very same day, and found two police officers in our kitchen, and Mum in what I think they describe as a very distressed state.

"It's Rupert," she said. She was in tears. "He's disappeared."

None of us had seen him since Saturday evening. He'd gone to Michael's, to work on a school project and to stay for the rest of the weekend. He'd taken night things and his school uniform in an overnight bag, and was supposed to have gone on to school with Michael today, Monday.

Only he hadn't. He'd gone to Michael's on Saturday, all right, but according to Michael's mum a cab had come to collect him at about nine o'clock. He told them he was wanted at home unexpectedly after all, and Michael's mum hadn't any reason to disbelieve him. It was the last anybody had seen of him.

But she'd obviously had some nagging doubt, and had telephoned Mum at work earlier that afternoon to tell her about it. It's how Mum found out he'd gone, otherwise she'd have been none the wiser until after school when he wouldn't have come home.

"I thought it was a bit strange," she'd told Mum, on the phone. "He didn't seem quite himself. He was – I don't know – agitated. And then when Mike came home for lunch and said Rupert wasn't at school today I thought he must be unwell. I thought I'd better ring to check he was OK."

Mum told us she hadn't known what to say, so she'd told Michael's mother that Rupert was perfectly fine, and had telephoned the police as soon as she had rung off.

"And why did you say that, Mrs Horton?" one of the policemen, the younger looking of the two, asked her. "Why did you tell Mrs Stewart that your stepson was all right? Why didn't you tell her you haven't seen him since he left here on Saturday afternoon?"

His tone was mild even if his words sounded unpleasantly insinuating. I rushed to where Mum was sitting limply at the table, and put my arms around her, protectively.

"Leave my mother alone!" I yelled. "Can't you see she's feeling dreadful enough as it is?"

"Of course," said the other policeman, smoothly. "No need to get upset. Now, if we could just go over it one more time, Mrs Horton?"

I found myself wishing, despite myself, that Geoffrey was there to handle the situation. *That old, helpless-female thing*. No, not because of that, I told myself, but because Mum would have drawn strength and comfort from his presence that she clearly wasn't getting from mine. And also because, at the end of the day, Rupert was his son.

"And you say your husband has gone away?"

"Yes. To America. On business, for three weeks."

"I see. And is there any chance he might have taken young Rupert with him?"

"What?" Mum stared at him, unseeing.

"Taken him? Of course not! I don't know what you mean!"

"Had you and your husband had any disagreements recently, maybe? Fallen out about anything?"

"You think Geoffrey's taken him as some kind of punishment for me," Mum stated, flatly. She spread out her hands on the table in front of her and regarded them dispassionately, as though they belonged to somebody else.

"We can't discount any possibility at this stage."

"You can discount that. Geoffrey would never do that, never. Why should he? Rupert's not even—"

Not even my son. The words rang out into the room, clearly, even though they hadn't been uttered. Mum shook her head, roughly, and then buried her face in her hands.

"Where's Molly?" I suddenly remembered her. I shook Mum by the shoulder. "Mum, where's Moll?"

"At Chloë's." Her voice was indistinct, muffled.

"And Molly is?" the younger policeman asked, pen poised over notebook.

"My sister. She's not going to know where Rupert is, she's only twelve."

I found myself telling the policemen that

280

Geoffrey had been gone since Saturday.

"Since Saturday?" They perked up, noticeably. "The same day Rupert went missing?"

"Yeah, but Geoffrey left here on Saturday morning, and Rupert didn't leave Michael's until nine that night. They're not together, I'm sure of it. Honestly."

"And your stepfather's gone to the States, on business?"

"That's right. Boston. He's an archaeologist, he's gone to do some lectures at the university." All of a sudden, I remembered something else. "But not until today. His flight went today, I'm sure that's what he said. Monday."

"So where did he go on Saturday?"

"To his mother's." Mum lifted her face from her hands. "He went to stay with his mother for a couple of days. She's elderly, he doesn't get to see her much."

"And where does she live?"

"Hounslow. Near Heathrow, you see. Handy for the airport."

In the end Mum rang Geoffrey's mother, she said the shock of having the police ringing and saying Rupert was missing might kill her. I don't know how Mum was so *au fait* with the elder Mrs Horton's health, as far as I was aware they'd never even met.

Anyway, everything had happened much as we'd thought.

"Geoffrey arrived after lunch on Saturday and left at eight thirty this morning," Mum said, putting the phone down. "No sign of Rupert. I didn't want to alarm her by telling her he was missing, so I just said I hoped she wasn't disappointed at not seeing him, too. She said she hadn't been expecting Rupert, he never went with Geoffrey on business trips — it was obvious he wasn't there, and never had been."

"I see."

I could tell from the policemen's faces they too were disappointed, that they'd been expecting Rupert to be at his grandmother's, sat in her lounge before a roaring fire, drinking orange squash and worn out from his little adventure. Or maybe that's what I'd hoped. I remembered his diary. *I begged him to let me go and stay with gran like I used to, but he says I can't.* I remembered his heartfelt words, the agonizing unhappiness bursting from the screen at the prospect of having to put up with us, the appalling Frys, for three weeks without his father's soothing presence. *I just can't bear it.*

"Actually," I said, slowly. "I think Rupert has gone to be with his father. I just don't think Geoffrey knows about it."

* * *

They found him at Heathrow, wandering around with his overnight bag, looking for a flight to Boston. They managed to page Geoffrey at Boston airport; he had to get straight on the next flight to London, without having time to have a meal or a sleep or even to check out.

We drove to Heathrow to pick them up. Mum insisted on that.

"I'm not having them coming back on the train," she kept saying. "It's the least I can do."

So we got up at six in the morning to drive the three hundred or so kilometres in Geoffrey's Volvo. I didn't mind. I was awake anyway. And Moll was pleased because she was missing a maths test.

All the way down I kept making silent bargains, inside my head, though with whom I didn't quite know. God, I suppose. *Let him be all right and I'll be nice to him for ever. Let him be all right and I'll tell him how sorry I am for having been such a cow. Let him be all right and I'll get Jaz to tell him she would really like to go out with him, but he's a bit young for her. Let him be all right...*

Nobody seemed to have the slightest notion what had happened to him in-between leaving Michael's on Saturday evening and being spotted at Heathrow at six o'clock on Monday evening, so his being all right certainly wasn't what you might call a foregone conclusion.

When we arrived at Heathrow we were met by a young woman who didn't look much older than me, dressed in a dark blue uniform skirt, coat and official-looking peaked cap. She ushered us through what seemed like kilometres of corridor and into a square, cream-painted box of a room. It had a blond wood coffee table with a tasteful display of lilies, and several low-slung black leather chairs.

"Do sit down," she said, capably, indicating the chairs with a sweep of her hand, "and I'll get someone to organize some coffees."

We were there for what seemed like an eternity, ignoring her invitation to sit and instead pacing restlessly up and down the room. It reminded me of some bears I'd seen once at the zoo, a long time ago, who'd paced their narrow enclosure and swung their heads mechanically, bored literally out of their minds. Only we weren't bored.

"God," said Molly, fiercely. "I'd rather be at school."

"I thought you said you had a maths test?"

"I'd still rather be at school."

Then all of a sudden the door swung open, and in came not some airport employee bearing a tray of coffee but Geoffrey, and behind him, Rupert. They were both deathly white, tired and drawn-looking with bruised hollows beneath their eyes. Geoffrey's chin was dark with two days' stubble, and Rupert looked unwashed, unkempt, his hair standing on end as if electrically charged. I had never in all my life been so glad to see anybody.

Mum made a little inarticulate noise and kind of stumbled towards them, putting her arms around them both and drawing them towards her, and for the first time I saw Rupert not as a deeply uncool individual, a smug self-satisfied alien being whose presence in our family threatened its very structure, but instead as what he was: a scared, unconfident, vulnerable little boy whose mother was dead.

I stood and watched my own mother embracing him and his father and I wanted to join in, wanted to show I understood why Rupert had gone missing and was sorry for my part in it, desperately sorry for having been so selfish. I wanted to promise them all I'd change, become a better person; but then I realized I didn't have to promise any such thing, because I already had changed.

epilogue

I read somewhere that adolescence has a lot in common with giving birth: after it's over, you forget about all the pain. Thank God you only have to go through adolescence once; is what I say. (Luckily, I have no experience of child-birth, though I suppose you don't have to go through that at all. Particularly if you're male.)

You see, I know what the shrinks would say. That I caused all the problems, or at least made them a whole lot worse. That I took against Rupert from the start, made him the scapegoat for my unhappiness at Geoffrey usurping my father's role. That I wanted to take up with my father again to punish my mother, that the whole thing with Sam was somehow con-nected, a — I don't know — a proclamation of my incipient adulthood and independence of my parents, or some such.

See? I've got all the jargon. And maybe they'd be right: maybe *I'm* right in my retrospective analysis of the situation. All I know is, it was bloody painful at the time. For all concerned. People told me I shouldn't blame myself for what happened, for Rupert and me not getting on and him running away. But I did blame myself, for a long time, and in a way I still do. How could I read his diary and *not* end up blaming myself? My suffering was all I could see: I couldn't recognize anybody else's pain. Certainly not Rupert's. Not Geoffrey's or Molly's. Not even Mum's – my mother, who I'd always considered myself so close to. Just self-centred little me and my feelings. And that's a hard lesson to learn about yourself. Anyway, who in the end gives a damn why it happened? It just did, and now it's over. And thank God for that.

Life goes on, as it does; didn't someone once say life is what happens when you're looking the other way? Sam is still kicking around school with what seems to be a different totty each week. He and Vanessa died a death pretty quickly. He did come on to Jaz, briefly, but she was having none of it. Think you can muck my best mate around and then wheedle your way round me? she told him. On yer bike. Or words to that effect. Bless.

Surprise of the century is Andy Cooper. For so long I'd just thought of him as Sam's slightly dopey sidekick, with no brains or character of his own to speak of. I suppose I was so dazzled by Golden Boy for so long that I had no eyes for anybody else. But guess what? Andy's not like that at all. In the aftermath of Sam and me, he was a — what's the old-fashioned word? A brick. If not an entire wall. Sam and Mattie Get Discovered in the Cupboard — it was, as I'd suspected, the talk of the school for a while. But Andy helped me to laugh about it, in public at any rate, and before long it had all been forgotten, just as he'd said it would. The latest goss is Sam and Jade Behind Stage During the School Production … you don't want to know. Trust me.

Yeah, yeah — I know. Sounds like Andy and me are an item now, doesn't it. But we're not. We're friends, is all. Proper friends. We talk, we have a laugh. It's what friends do — friends aren't bothered about having a snog or groping each other. Mind you, I'm not ruling it out. Not entirely. But it will be a long time, post-Sam, before I'm ready for any more of that kind of thing. I've gone right off sex-on-a-stick type men.

Even things at home are better. Not brilliant; just better. Nobody is pretending stepfamilies are easy things to get used to, which oddly enough seems to help in itself. Mum has stopped wafting around, acting as if everything's tickety-boo and it's only a matter of time before Rupert and I are in each other's pockets. I guess that makes it sound as if I'm blaming Mum, and I truly don't mean to. But difficult situations aren't made easier by pretending the difficulties don't exist.

As for Rupert, he's left St Mark's and is now at another private school that Geoffrey says can cope better with his needs. He says it was a mistake sending him to St Mark's in the first place, that it was throwing us all in together at the deep end and was asking for problems. His actual words. (Geoffrey, acknowledging a problem; apparently Mum's not the only one being a whole lot more realistic about things.)

Anyway, Rupert; he's what's called a weekly boarder, which basically means he's at school during the week and comes home Friday evenings for the weekends. He's not nearly such a pain now when he's home. Partly because he virtually lives round at Michael's, but partly because of the way he is now. He seems different, kind of. Don't get me wrong: he still looks the same. Spotty, specky. Geeky and gawky. Brad Pitt he ain't. But somehow – this is going to sound dead cheesy, but I'm going to say it anyway– somehow, it's as though he's different inside. His eyes have changed, they don't look superior and sneery any more, but alive and interested. Perhaps he's happy now. (I know I am – or happier, at any rate.) I suppose everyone deserves some happiness in their lives. Even Rupert. It's like what he wanted in his story has really happened: Ty'n Grhyn has gone, and Roo P't has taken his place. And the Bitch-Queen M'Atil Da'aa has been vanquished, never to be seen again... We're quite civilized towards each other now, we even exchange conversation over the supper table. Amazing. Admittedly it's usually confined to the please-pass-the-salt variety, but it's a start.

I guess we're all happier now. Like I said, life goes on. Cliché cliché.

HARD CASH

Kate Cann

My name's Rich. Which is funny, because at this moment I have only 72p in the pocket of my worn out jacket and no prospect of getting my hands on any more until Friday. I can't afford clothes. I can't afford booze. I can't afford anything. Every single one of my art pencils needs replacing and I can't afford that, either. I daren't even sharpen the bloody things when I need to now. If they get much shorter I'll be holding them with tweezers.

Money. It does your head in. Not having it, I mean.

I saw this bloke on the way home tonight. He was one-handedly trying to park his brand-new BMW convertible in a very narrow space and all the time he was jerking back and forth he was jabbering into this flashy little silver mobile. I stood there, in the shadow of the tree by my gate, and stared at him, and my stomach went into this tight hot knot of hate and envy.

He jammed the car to a stop, not straight, as though it wouldn't really matter if someone took his sidelight off because he could always get another sidelight – or another car – and jumped out. Everything about him gave off money vibrations. His suit, his shoes, the way his hair was cut, the way his body and face were a little bit plump but still shining and toned, like he ate and drank very well but then worked it off at some high-tech gym afterwards.

He went round to the boot of the car and hauled out a classy-looking sports bag, two carriers from one of those late-night top-price delis, and a bunch of lilies. Then he slammed the boot shut, locked it with a noisy remote, and headed off across the street.

I stared after him, and I wanted to kill him. You sleek bastard. You're going to leg it into your smart flat and whip up whatever designer-foody goodies you have stashed in that bag and then some top bird is going to come round and you'll pop some champagne and give her the lilies and she'll end up shagging you with all her silky clothes chucked around the place. And the real pain of it is this is just normal workaday stuff for you. This is life.

And I can't even afford a couple of sodding pencils.

To the rich shall be given more – all the food all the cars all the booze all the birds yeah even until the ending of the earth.

And the poor had just better get over it.

"Be grateful you've got a roof over your head and food on the table," Mum always says. With a look that implies that I'm an ungrateful git. Which I probably am. I walk up our path and let myself into our skinny little hall that's needed redecorating for five years and more. Every spring, Dad makes some joke like, "Why don't you do it, Richard? You're supposed to be able to paint." And I think maybe I should, but I don't ever get round to it.

"Mum?"

"In here, luv. In the kitchen."

"What's for supper?"

"Spag bol."

"Great, Mum. I'm starved."

"When aren't you? Grate me up that cheese, luv."

We don't have proper Parmesan on our spag bol. We have old Cheddar that Mum gets cheap from the market. It's OK – smells as bad. She does OK with the pathetically small amount she has to spend on food each week.

They're proud of how well they budget, my parents. To hear them talk, you'd think budgeting was every bit as good as having money.

Dad walks through the door and looks at me in the raised-chin, challenging way he's used ever since I got more or less sanely past puberty. Dad challenges most people, especially men, and Mum says he could've got a lot further in his line of work if he didn't do it quite so much. But he says it's better to be hard up and keep your pride. Maybe he's right.

"So how was college, son?" he asks.

"Oh, OK. Got bollocked by Huw again."

"Why?"

"Late assignment."

"Good God, d'you ever do an assignment you don't give in late?"

I shrug. "It was a crap topic."

"He's the teacher, son, not you. If he sets you a topic it's because you need it for your grades."

"I don't see what drawing a pile of lemons and crap has to do with anything."

"Nor do I, but if he sets it, you do it, right?"

"Leave him alone, Bill," says Mum tiredly.

"Yeah, leave me alone, Dad," I say. Sometimes I think he just asks me stuff so he can jump on something and lecture me about it. He's on my back the whole time. It does my head in if you want the truth.

"Call Sam for me," Mum says to Dad.

"It'll be ready in five minutes." Dad stomps out to the hall to yell up the stairs or my little brother Sam, and Mum says, "Work isn't the only reason you're fed up, is it?"

I shrug.

"You still mooning after that girl?"

I shrug again. I could shrug for England, I reckon.

"I don't know, Rich. Why don't you just ask her out?"

" 'Cos she'd say no."

"Course she wouldn't. Good-looking boy like you."

"I can't afford to ask her out."

"Good God, you'd think feminism had never happened. Girls don't expect to get paid for nowadays."

"Girls like Portia McCutcheon do."

Mum dips her mouth in the way that says, "She's not worth it then."

Maybe she isn't, but I'll never get the chance to find out, will I?"

Sam bursts in talking to Dad about football, just like I used to do, and we all sit down and eat and Dad tells me to cheer up and I hate myself for being so miserable and sour. It's not my folks' fault they're not rich. They're great – well, Mum is – loads better than some of the jerks I see letting themselves in and out of the remote-controlled gates of the posh tenements just up our street. It's just—

My parents are the salt of the earth and yes salt glitters but not like diamonds do.

I had a job two months ago. It lasted three weeks. I worked two nights, sometimes three, in this bar in town. It was brilliant. OK pay, free food, free beer – that's what did me in, of course. I liked the beer too much. And I got totally pissed once too often and got fired, with no hope of a reference. Not that there were any others jobs to go for. Bar jobs are like gold dust in this place.

Sam has a paper round. The little sod's a lot richer than I am and what's he got to spend it on? Chewing gum and hair gel, that's all. The odd trip to lie his way into a 15 movie. I've considered asking him for a loan but, Christ, you've got to have some pride.

Last week Dad said I could do the sweeping up Saturdays at his factory and got very short with me when I turned it down. Pride again. But I mean, *me* – sweeping up?

Anyway it was OK to turn it down because I've got a plan. Mum still slips me a few quid every Friday, about a fiver, whatever she can afford. And this Friday I'm spending it on stamps. I've already blagged five big A2 envelopes out of the stationery cupboard outside the Art Department. And I've got five sets of six of my top drawings – I managed to photocopy them when the office was empty of all but Charlotte, who thinks I'm a "nice boy" because I don't have excess body-piercing like most of the art lot.

These drawings are – they're good. Even Huw said they're good. "Christ, though, boy," he said. "Look at the pain in these. Look at the barely-repressed rage. We should get you some therapy. Mind you, if these scribbles are indications of your inner being, what therapist would knowingly go anywhere near it?"

Ha, ha. Huw reckons he's a real funny man. My pictures are pretty dark though. Monsters and ghouls and nightmares. But they're *strong*. They come off the page at you, alive — more alive than most stuff in the real world. I love them and I loved doing them. And now I'm sending them out to try to make myself some money.

I've done the research. I've got the names of five little local companies — three advertising, two graphic design. With the help of Charlotte I've written out five really good letters, that stop just this side of actual begging, saying, This is a sample of my work and I'll do anything for you, anything at all.

I can hear you saying I haven't got a hope in hell. I can hear you saying, You'd have better odds if you spent your money on lottery tickets, not stamps.

Yeah, well, maybe you're right, but I've got to try, right? I'm desperate.